Praise for *M...*

'A remarkable achievement, ...ty and an absorbing and very personal experience, like reading someone's beautifully poetic and honest diary.' *Meanjin*

'The pleasures of bathing, cycling, Paris and song are threaded through memories of unrequited love, unrealised longing and lovers.' *Canberra Times*

'*My Hundred Lovers* is an original imagining of one woman's waning flesh and the vibrant imprint of a life it still holds.' *The Age*

Praise for *The Broken Book*

'Both very Australian and resoundingly international, *The Broken Book* confirms Johnson's status as one of the finest Australian writers . . . fiercely beautiful.' *The Australian*

'A bold narrative, in which we're constantly reminded by the quality of her prose that this is an imaginative work . . . It's a kaleidoscope of memory, jagged and disordered as the artist's tragic life.' *Canberra Times*

Praise for *Life in Seven Mistakes*

'Feeling, insight, rambunctious wit.' *New York Times Book Review*

'She has a knack for presenting what can be unbearable in reality, of rendering it on the page with tremendous heart.' *Sydney Morning Herald*

Susan Johnson was shortlisted for the 1991 Victorian Premier's Literary Award for her novel *Flying Lessons*, shortlisted for the 1994 National Book Council's Banjo Award for the novel *A Big Life* and shortlisted for the National Biography Award 2000 for her memoir *A Better Woman*. Her other books include *Hungry Ghosts*, *Messages from Chaos*, *Women Love Sex* (editor and contributor) and *Life in Seven Mistakes*. *The Broken Book* was shortlisted for the 2005 Nita B Kibble Award, the Best Fiction Book section of the Queensland Premier's Literary Award, the Westfield/Waverley Library Literary Award, and the Australian Literary Society Gold Medal Award for an Outstanding Australian Literary Work. Her last novel, *My Hundred Lovers*, was published in 2012 to critical acclaim.

In 2010 she returned from ten years in London to live in Brisbane. She is a feature writer at *Qweekend* magazine.

ALSO BY SUSAN JOHNSON

FICTION

Latitudes: New Writing from the North (co-editor, 1986)
Messages from Chaos (1987)
Flying Lessons (1990)
A Big Life (1993)
Women Love Sex (editor, 1996)
Hungry Ghosts (1996)
The Broken Book (2004)
Life in Seven Mistakes (2008)
My Hundred Lovers (2012)

NON-FICTION

A Better Woman (1999)
On Beauty (2009)

The Landing

Susan Johnson

ALLEN&UNWIN

SYDNEY · MELBOURNE · AUCKLAND · LONDON

First published in 2015

  This project has been assisted by the Australian
Government through the Australia Council,
its arts funding and advisory board.

Australian Government

Allen & Unwin
83 Alexander Street
Crows Nest NSW 2065
Australia
Phone: (61 2) 8425 0100
Email: info@allenandunwin.com
Web: www.allenandunwin.com

Cataloguing-in-Publication details are available
from the National Library of Australia
www.trove.nla.gov.au

ISBN 978 1 76011 393 3

Design by Sandy Cull, gogoGingko
Typeset in 13.5/18 pt Perpetua by Bookhouse, Sydney
Printed and bound in Australia by Griffin Press

1 3 5 7 9 10 8 6 4 2

For Sandra Hogan, encore, friend of my heart
And for Jeff Humphreys, who is loved

A novel—a small tale, generally of love.

DR SAMUEL JOHNSON,
A Dictionary of the English Language

All the conventions conspire
To make this fort assume
The furniture of home;
Lest we should see where we are,
Lost in a haunted wood,
Children afraid of the night
Who have never been happy or good.

W.H. AUDEN,
'September 1, 1939'

PART

|

ONE

A new wife

If a separated man—about to be divorced—is in possession of a good fortune, must he be in want of a new wife? Jonathan Lott was fifty-five years old and almost a free man, despite his reluctance to relinquish the phrase 'my wife', which he had continued to use throughout the two sad years of his separation, even though that nominal wife had run off with a woman. What woman suddenly decides she bats for the other team at the advanced age of forty-six, two children behind her? When Jonathan thought of Sarah now, he thought of her not just as a loss to himself but as a loss to men: her crooked mouth, her tawny loveliness, still tawny, still lovely, though no longer young. He recalled the first time he entered the grandiose dining room of the Brisbane Club, that tall-ceilinged, hallowed place, after Sarah left him—silencing the room or else causing it to erupt into titters or whispers and *sotto voce* alerts, he can no longer remember which—as one of the bravest moments of his life.

Everyone was talking about him, *everyone*, and yet he walked in. Which senior partner of a prestigious city firm specialising in construction law ever endured such a public humiliation? Blokes either got caught with their pants down or their wives cuckolded them with their business partners or else they went broke or ran off with inappropriate young women—like Paul Raymond, who left his wife for his neighbours' daughter, nineteen-year-old Scarlett Collins, the prettiest girl in The Landing, that modest settlement by the great natural lake where Jonathan had a holiday house. Jonathan thought perhaps the only thing Sarah could have done to scandalise the good citizens of The Landing or the Brisbane Club more was to run off with a pretty nineteen-year-old boy waiter.

The Landing was a slender tip of a finger of God's earth extending out into a magnificent lake, part of a pleasing system of waterways made up of beaches, rivers and fresh and shallow saltwater lakes one hundred and fifty kilometres north of Brisbane. With a population of two hundred and twenty souls, it was a small but proud part of that lucky corner of south-east Queensland, the part growing faster than any other place in the country, attracting newcomers as if there were a goldrush or a mining boom. (As it happened there *was* a mining boom, but way out west, in that unglamorous sunbaked country where the questing residents of Toorak or Point Piper never ventured.)

Only a few of these newcomers knew about The Landing, nestled as it was in the hinterland of the more glamorous coast, down a perilous bit of road, slightly too far from the restaurants and bars of Noosa's Hastings Street. It was hillbilly in comparison: a few streetlights and a couple of bitumen roads, kerbed and guttered, but slow and erratic internet and mobile phone coverage and definitely no reticulated water and sewage. There wasn't even a fashionable coffee shop roasting organic coffee beans exclusively hand-harvested from Honduras Monte Escondido Estate or the remote highlands of Papua New Guinea. The only place to go at The Landing was the Orpheus Hotel, built during that other mining boom, the gold rush of the mid-1800s, and once famous as Nash's Orpheus Philharmonic Music Hall Hotel.

Jonathan did not like to think of himself as winded by love, but he sometimes thought of those first days after Sarah left him, when he lay gasping in his bed, his heart trying to leap free from the cage of his body. He supposed these were panic attacks, these wild thrashings in the night, when the pump of his own blood seemed to wake him. He could hear the circuitry of his own animation as it were, the tracery of artery and nerve, which only the net of his own skin seemed to prevent from exploding. He had a vision of flying apart into pieces like one of those science experiments, released from the laws of physics and the motions of bodies, his own humbled workings and all the celestial bodies in space, blown, torn, scattered. Sometimes, back then, even when he was wide awake and walking, he had a physical sensation of listing to one side, and had to lean against walls to steady himself. In those early days he suspected a brain tumour or motor neurone disease, some lurking malignancy, trying to fell him. Now, in the car speeding north, Jonathan was loosening his grip on the grief of his impending divorce (which, Sarah had declared the day before, they should get around to finalising), on the pile of building reports and investigations into toxic waste on the Cardwell site, on the emails from women who had designs on him.

Already he could see the Glasshouse Mountains in the distance, named by that homesick Yorkshireman Captain James Cook for their resemblance to the glass-making furnaces and kilns of his native shire. The monstrous hulking mass of Mount Tibrogargan rising still thrilled Jonathan, as it had as a small child. One of his few pleasant memories of his irascible father was driving along the old highway and his dad telling him that the mountain was all that remained of an ancient fossilised gorilla and Jonathan being young enough to believe him. Jonathan could still make out the shape of the ape's great shoulders and head every time he passed it. On a whim, he turned off the new highway onto the old, just so he could see it again. The mountain's glacial patience rarely failed to induce a quietening of the incessant chatter and clang within his greying head. Who has not wished to quiet the clatter, to start afresh, renewed, awakened? Who hasn't yearned to have one's life spread out once more, a ribbon of endless hope? The great mountain and the ranges behind, the white-sand beaches beyond and the tempting dream were upon Jonathan now, the feeling that somewhere, sometime, he would find a beautiful sanctuary of infinite joy and rest.

The good citizens of The Landing—and even the not-so-good—were universally agreed that The Landing was indeed a peaceful refuge in the wake of relentless life. Jonathan felt it on the impossibly long winding road off the highway that led into The Landing at the moment when he flicked the switch to lower the Audi's four windows, when the smell of lantana and gum trees and salt air rushed in, together with the squall of white cockatoos and grey and pink galahs, kookaburras, crows, butcherbirds, cicadas, so noisy, so clear, so freeing. He felt it at the first sight of that wide, sweeping view over the trees and across to the The Landing and the vast lake fed by the river, in its turn fed by the sea. Beyond, beyond, ancient sand dunes and, finally, the great swell of the Pacific Ocean, its endless depths spreading halfway across the earth.

Jonathan took his eyes off the road for a moment to take in that first sight of the ocean. He felt his body unclenching and noticed the slow spread of ease down his neck and across his shoulders. Might he—after all—survive the failure of love? And had his love really been a failure? He wasn't ready yet to think of suitable candidates to replace the love that had for so long been at the heart of his life, despite the apparently endless stream of women figuratively offering to mend his socks. His mind turned to Rosanna, the cast-off wife of Paul Raymond, who ran off with Scarlett, but immediately veered away. He pictured Penny Collins, Scarlett's embittered, once-beautiful mother, who might be awakened by a kiss—as, indeed, so might he. Did he even need a new wife when he was so stupidly and mistakenly attached to the old?

TWO

Ariadne's thread

But even paradise feels landlocked to some: to Penny Collins, for example, the divorced mother of The Prettiest Girl in The Landing. Not so long ago Penny herself had been the prettiest girl and also, not so long ago, she had taken herself off, secretly, to an expensive room on Hastings Street, where she lay upon a virginal white sheet and had poison injected into the skin around her eyes and her forehead. Botulism was it? Bacteria? In truth, Penny Collins did not really care what Botox was, except that she hoped it might act like the hand of God, stretching out to stop time. Recently Penny caught herself relishing the idea that even her beauteous daughter, Scarlett, would grow old, even though Scarlett, like everyone young, did not believe this would ever happen to her. Penny accepted Freud's theory that in the unconscious everyone was convinced of his own immortality.

Penny had once been the most brilliant art student at her small private Brisbane girls' school, a favourite of the art teacher, who awarded her the school art prize and who predicted she was marked for great things. Penny left St Margaret's in a blaze of glory, a celebrated figure, with an overheated idea about becoming a good artist—even a great one. But perhaps her ambition outweighed her abilities, or else her perfectionist's unappeasable eye scuttled what talent she had, for at art college she soon discovered she was no longer the best student—and indeed could not even capture the attention of her teachers. The star students were making conceptual multimedia installations, featuring themselves, or photographing holes in the bitumen of roads, and she was left behind with her paints and figure drawings and nineteenth-century ideas about beauty, which no-one applauded any longer. She was full of self-doubt, forced to recognise that a modicum of talent got you so far and no further, and that while she had imagined she was climbing the mountain, in truth she was only ever at the bottom.

These days, while Penny did not feel herself to be inhabiting the wrong life, not exactly, she felt herself to be in not quite the right place. Her life was made, and she had made it, though she frequently blamed her reliably negative ex-husband, Pete. She had sent him a postcard from her recent visit to the Freud Museum in London. *It's Never Too Late to Have a Happy Childhood*, the postcard read and she signed her name and drew a happy face beside it. After Freud and his family fled the Nazis, Freud had re-created his Viennese consulting room in the house. On the day of her visit, the famous psychoanalytic couch was draped in a richly coloured Iranian rug, and in the dark room an American woman was weeping openly at the sight of it. Penny thought the woman hysterical; she herself was at the house mainly because of Sigmund's grandson, the late painter Lucian.

Penny was there in the hope of tracing the line of prodigious talent—Freud's thickly strewn paint, not strewn in actuality but laid on precisely, truer than flesh, the corpulence of the bodies, spreading out to the edges not only of themselves but to the painting and beyond—for she had once wanted this painting truth for herself. Not so long ago, she had yearned to follow the Ariadne's thread that would guide her to that point of release where she could express whatever was original in her, that shining point which would allow her to arrange her feelings of fear and wonder, without having to suffer for it, as in life. She wished to breach the disjunction between the forensic acuity with which she comprehended existence—the inchoate mess of tender understanding within her, for her husband and their lost life together, for her ruined daughter, Scarlett, for her maddening, impossible mother, Marie—with the silence that choked her. Penny suspected every human soul shared a desire for expression but, instead of comforting her, this suspicion only made her feel pinched and bad-tempered. She lived with her best words stranded in her throat but, unlike most, the painter Lucian Freud had learned to speak them.

The London visit was Penny's third trip to Europe. The first had been as a young backpacker who still believed the adolescent dream of destiny, that she had marvellous things of interest within her, her greatness clothed, as yet unrevealed. The second trip, at twenty-five, was a year-long tilt at becoming a serious artist, spent mostly in France, her mother's birthplace and what she hoped would prove her real home too. But nothing went as planned and she returned, as if waking from a dream, some veil of understanding beginning to be parted, the queasy doubts and concessions of humble, disappointing adulthood becoming faintly visible in the dimness ahead. Her most recent trip to London and the Freud Museum was spur of the moment, booked in a huff when she had grown fed up with seeing Scarlett and her two children—both under three—day after day. Scarlett, dumb to her ruined life! Penny felt overwhelmed by the conflicting pull of serves-Scarlett-bloody-well-right revenge and oh-God-she's-wasted-her-life pity. How had Penny ended up a bit player in a Freudian drama not of her own fucking making? How had she produced a daughter who clearly had such an enormous daddy complex that she ran away—admittedly not very far—with a man six years older than her own father? Scarlett's father and Penny's disappointing ex-husband, Pete, still lived at The Landing, but Penny remained at the family home, next door to that abandoned wife, Rosanna Raymond. It was Rosanna's husband, Paul—loud, big-gutted, big drinking—who ran off with Scarlett, now twenty-three and the harassed mother of Ajax and Hippolyte. Penny recalled the many sacrifices she had made for her daughter: the fights with Pete about sending her to a private church school instead of the local state high school (peopled by morons and ratbags), the ridiculous fees, the guilt loan from her mother, years of driving forty kilometres to drop Scarlett by the side of the highway to meet the school bus, then turning the car around and driving forty kilometres back to her own job as a high school art teacher. And for what?

Now Penny lived with the injustice of seeing not only Scarlett and her offspring every day but Pete, too, and fat-gutted

Paul and Paul's cast-off wife, who, like Penny, remained in the family home but who, unlike Penny, remained smiling. Penny did not understand Rosanna: it was galling enough for Penny to endure Friday nights at the Orpheus, seeing her impulsive, dim-witted daughter slow dancing to 'The First Time Ever I Saw Your Face' with her balding partner, but how could Rosanna stand it? If Paul were her husband, Penny would never again have spoken to him after the violent manner in which he had left a twenty-five-year marriage, withdrawing all their joint money and running off to live in Paris for six months with a pregnant teenage girl. How could Rosanna remain upright? Yet there she was, fifty-three years old, the same age as Penny, wearing a little short dress of the kind that girls wore these days, like a child's dress, a scrap of cotton held up by two threads at each shoulder. Rosanna, of hopeful temperament, dancing alone at the Orpheus, a deranged, blissed-out hippy smile on her face, holding her age well, not because of Botox or a healthy diet, but because of a fluke of genetics. Rosanna smoked. Rosanna drank too much. Rosanna's face was unlined except for a fan of wrinkles around her eyes, which encouraged a view that she was a happy, contented kind of person.

Every morning in the milky yellow dawn, before the wind rose, Rosanna walked down to the brown shallow lake to swim, way past the scummy, soggy bottom that discouraged new swimmers, their feet sinking as if into slime, and out into the deeper water with its unseen sandy bottom, right out to where the sailing boats flew by, the early-morning kayaks, the rowers, the fishermen checking their crab pots, the occasional small fish briefly skimming upright across the surface of the unruffled dawn water. She swam among the ospreys, kites and white herons, among fish gently breaking the skin of the water, leaving perfect concentric circles radiating outwards. Rosanna swam on her back in shimmering light, opening her eyes to the creamy swirl of dawn clouds against the brightening sky, a single morning star still sparkling, the water indivisible from the sky, turning the whole world into liquid silver, letting her arms, her legs, her fingers and toes open out into the universe. It was so still, so quiet, she could hear the surf from the far side of the lake, from over the dunes and across the sands, smashing up from the ocean, reaching her ears like the sound of a distant jet. Rosanna was free. Rosanna refused to hold on to her pain. Rosanna had let everything go because forgiveness is a choice not to suffer.

THREE

The wrong side of the lake

On the far eastern bank, opposite the settlement known as The Landing, the world's oldest sand dunes separate the immense lake from the ocean. Laced and tethered to the earth by fleshy-leaved, purple-flowered pigface, goat's foot vine and spinifex, held safe from the wind, the dunes rise up from the clean sweep of beach facing the ocean. Behind them runs a heath, scrubby with low-lying pandanus and other hardy plants, which in turn becomes a scribbled forest of melaleuca trees, wrinkled, grey, ghostly. Sprinkled throughout are spiny, needle-like grass trees and sweet-nectared yellow banksias, bursting and round as pompoms, and native fungi, brilliant red, curled like sea anemone or bright orange, leaping like frozen licks of flame.

At his holiday house on the western edge of the lake, at 36 Waratah Street, Jonathan was opening up. It had been months since Jonathan's last visit and the air inside smelled trapped, old, and he passed from room to room, opening windows, so that freshness rushed in, the scent of trees. It was a brand-new house, a year old, and a Sarah-free zone; a project they had originally planned together but which Sarah had never seen completed. She had chosen the architect: a rising star who happened to be the daughter of his best friend, Will, and only a few years older than their own daughters, Madeleine and Amanda. Sarah had sketched out rough designs and when she left him, in the middle of their lives, in the middle of their plans not only for a new holiday house but in the very movement of life itself—or so it seemed to him—he had stalled. At first he did nothing, apart from asking Sarah what she wanted to do about the house, to which she replied, 'Oh, for God's sake. Can't you decide?' And so he pressed on, to distract himself from pain, choosing bench tops and vanity basins and the colour of floorboards, everything Sarah would have done. He and Sarah still shared joint accounts; she was not interested in how much the house cost—and its costs were considerable—for she had never cared about money, and now she did not have to care, being an only child who some years before had inherited her widowed mother's multi-million-dollar estate.

The new house was built on one of The Landing's rare waterfront blocks, on the street running around the western edge of the lake, considered the best street in the village. The house featured glass, corrugated iron and sober, modernist angles. It sat in a cul-de-sac, tucked away amid the trees. The only sounds were birds, wind and water, and the occasional cries of windsurfers or men rigging their sailing skiffs; the knock of metal against the masts of moored, drifting boats. Jonathan's front lawn ran right down to the lake itself, to the rushes and reeds growing in the soft sands and water, where he had planted native waterlilies, purple and white, floating among the fat glossy leaves on the surface of the water. The lake was now a sailing hub, because of the reliable high winds which blew up most afternoons—and less often in the mornings—gusting among the trees around the house, tossing their leaves about in frantic chatter. On some nights, the many trees around the property shook and rattled throughout the long black hours, the brittle gums, the rustling pines planted more than one hundred years ago by an old bushie, one of The Landing's first white settlers. The land originally belonged to the Gubbi Gubbi people, who feasted on the animals of the lake and the sea—dugong and eels, black swan and other water fowl.

Jonathan could have made a bit of money renting out the house, particularly in high season when the sailing regattas were on. But he enjoyed the idea of a house just for him, a house cleaned and ready and waiting only for his key in the lock. The cleaner was the aged mother of the owner of The Landing's only shop, who ran the shop and much else besides as if he were a mobster and the village his fiefdom. Jonathan did not much like Phil Watson and his enormous, slatternly, chain-smoking wife, Sylvia, known as Sylv; nor did he like the idea of Phil's gossipy, hard-bitten old biddy of a mother, Phyllis, snooping about his house. She had a face shaped like a bent shoe, her large jaw curled as if rushing to meet the tip of her nose. It was the face of a wicked witch in a children's story and Jonathan was both repelled and oddly fascinated. He had once brought a woman up for a disastrous weekend, a leggy divorcee with a son at Grammar, who turned out to have a drinking problem and who told him soon after they arrived that she much preferred Straddie, where all the other Grammar parents had beach houses and where *everyone* went, and which she declared to be 'very, very social'. Phyllis rang his office first thing Monday morning to tell him the leggy divorcee had left something behind. 'She left her flirties,' she said, and instead of posting them to his home, as requested, she sent a pair of lacy crotchless knickers—with no accompanying note—to his office, where his secretary opened the envelope.

When all the windows were open, the house felt empty, full of echoes; at once Jonathan decided to wander out later and see who he could rustle up for a barbecue the following night. But first he put on a Miles Davis CD, opened a good bottle of red and took the bottle and a glass out onto the veranda. The veranda was high up in the trees, like a treehouse. The trees made a clearing, revealing his little private beach with its waterlilies below, the slap of frilly waves joining the leaves jostled by the wind, together making a sound like rushing water. There was the rattle of metal against metal; the flap of unseen sails on craft out on the water. The lake, spread out, always moving, never quiet except for sweet moments in still, noiseless dawns; dark and glossy beneath the late-afternoon sun. The wind was rising now, shaking the trees, whipping the leaves and lifting his hair. Jonathan was growing it; he still had a full head, silver now, but thick, abundant. He was vain about his hair, pleased to have it blowing about his face—attractively, he hoped. He was vain about his figure, too, long and tall and rangy like his late father, and free of the little pregnant belly Will and other men his age carried tenderly before them. If there were no mirrors in the world Jonathan might suppose himself to be the same man he was at twenty-nine, standing in the leafy garden of his parents' Clayfield house, marrying Sarah. His hair was long then, too, but dark, romantic. He had black eyebrows, straight as an artist's line of paint, and full lips Sarah called 'adorably kissable'. Sarah, aged twenty-two, with her lopsided smile! She was exuberance itself, a portal for joy, a great, whooshing rush of life, sweeping up friends and admirers and lecturers and bosses and him, him, him. Sarah had pinned him to existence, tracing all the points of his circumference, filling him in like a map. It was the saddest day of his life when he finally supposed her love for him had been extinguished. 'I got married too young,' she said. 'I didn't know who I was.' He looked up at the sky now, at the faint glow of emerging stars, bright stains against the sky's cloth, and, not for the first time, felt bewildered. I am still alive, he thought. What am I to do now?

The birds woke him, noisier than a schoolyard: two kooka- burras led the charge, followed by a string of notes like a chime, a whistle, some curly ascending scales, whipbirds, the squawking of cockatoos and parrots and, at the centre of it all, the two loud-mouthed kookaburras, calling and answering. It was that bright moment just before dawn, the flush of light coming into the world, a tender beam of radiance. He lay in bed as the world emerged like a developing film, the chair, the end of the bed; the room his photographic darkroom. He had deliberately left the shutters open, pulled back to each side of the wide window overlooking the swoop of the lake. Already, in the pre-dawn, the shutters were beginning to chatter, rattling softly in their tracks. A gecko on the ceiling emitted a comforting tick. It was late September, spring, the days not yet putrefying in the Queensland summer heat.

Jonathan rose eagerly from the bed, restored by the birds and the dawn. He threw on a T-shirt and a pair of jeans, and opened the back door to find Bites, the village dog. A big, dopey golden retriever, she wagged her tail at the sight of him. Bites liked to follow random men, slavishly, devotedly. 'Morning, Bites,' he said. 'How's it hanging?' Possibly this was not the appropriate question to ask a bitch, but she appeared to forgive him, looking up with love-struck eyes. She belonged to old Gordie, a retired doctor, a Scot, from up the road, one of the many retirees who lived full-time in the village, alongside dozens of old hippies: men who had smoked too many spliffs, their feet bare and their greying hair in scraggly ponytails; women with tanned skin wrinkled from the sun, pieces of aged coloured cotton around their wrists, wearing Balinese sarongs, teaching yoga or offering a safe space in which to experience past-life regression therapy. Anyone young, or youngish, and still working travelled to jobs at one of the small towns close by; only a handful had work requiring them to travel as far as Brisbane. At just under a two-hour drive (or one and a half if you mercifully escaped the traffic and floored it), The Landing was considered a tad too far to be within the city's commuter belt.

A good number of houses at The Landing were left empty or leased as holiday rentals, and some belonged to wealthy barristers, cardiac specialists, ear-nose-and-throat men, property developers and CEOs who, like Jonathan, used them as occasional weekenders. Not all were as swish as his house: a few dated from The Landing's beginnings as an early-twentieth-century holiday spot, when farmers and working men knocked up what amounted to barely more than shacks, some built of the softwood timbers from forests further inland but most made of poisonous asbestos, requiring specially trained men in masks to take walls down when it came to renovating them.

Jonathan and Sarah had been coming for years, on and off, and he could still pick out all the houses they had rented when he believed they were happy, when Madeleine and Amanda were little and the lake was perfect for two small, paddling girls; when unsporty Amanda surprised them in the summer she turned ten by becoming—briefly—enamoured of sailing. Because the community was small and everyone knew everyone, they had come to be regarded as regulars; they had friends they caught up with every summer and now everyone knew better than to mention his fugitive, soon-to-be-ex-wife.

Accompanied by the genial Bites, Jonathan walked down the back steps of his house, past the rustling bushes beginning to be tickled by the wind, down through his long garden and out into the street. The light was pearly; up ahead he saw that the newly erected shower and toilet block, still unfinished on his last visit, was now open. This facility had been championed by Phil from the shop, unofficial mayor and vice-president to Sylv's presidential role at The Landing Progress Association. Several members were unhappy to have the overbearing husband-and-wife team ruling the roost, but no-one could find a clause in the rules which forbade it. 'They probably wrote the bloody rule book,' said old Gordie; he had once been a member of the association but had resigned in protest over the Stalinist dictatorship of the Watsons.

Jonathan wondered if there had been a ceremony, with pompous Sylv in all her hefty glory cutting a ribbon, declaring the dunny open. Out of curiosity, he ventured inside: the doors were swung wide, revealing stainless-steel toilets—flushing he noted and not compost toilets like those in the camping ground. *See Sylv for a good time*, some wit had already written above the sink, alongside *Chrissy is a slag*. Big news for The Landing, he thought, as Bites gave the back of his calf a lover's lick. 'Outside,' he said. 'Come on, Bites.'

On the bright new flag of white cement outside the toilet block, edged upon the scrappy grass like icing on a cake, a little drawing made in pink chalk stood out. Designed as a hopscotch, words and drawings lay within the squares rather than numbers. *This is me*, the first square read, followed by an image of a stick figure, with rather alarming curly hair emerging from its head. *My name is Giselle. I am seven*, said the words in consecutive squares below the stick figure, then *My fafit food is*. He couldn't make out the next words. Cheese was it? Chips? Whatever it was, the child could not spell it.

This is me. He marvelled at the audacity of it.

FOUR

Power walking

Penny was up early too, power walking around the lake, feeling the wind against her cheeks and rushing under her arms as she swung them. She was lengthening her stride, conscious of the big muscles of her thighs, the stretch of her hamstrings. She refused to wear exercise clothing, to bestow free advertising on a new lycra range, names emblazoned over everything. Since when did 'fitness' become a hobby, something you listed as an interest on an internet dating site? If she saw another new mother dressed by Lorna Jane, slimmer than a twelve-year-old, jogging around the lake while pushing a specially designed three-wheel pram containing an infant less than two months old, she would trip her up. Penny wore an old T-shirt of Pete's, which still carried the shape of his body, and a stained pair of shorts she now used only for gardening. Running shoes were a different matter: she wore a pair of top-of-the-range Nikes, fluorescent orange, necessary to support the healed bone in her foot (embarrassingly broken falling off her new high-heeled shoes while dancing at the Orpheus. Oh, age, where is thy mercy?). She was scared of decay, of dissembling, of losing her shaky place in the world and ending up like her friendless, embattled mother. Marie—whom she never called 'Mum'—lived unhappily in a retirement village, having failed to manipulate either of her two daughters into living with her. Marie made enemies of everyone, her only pleasure derived from flirting with hapless ancient gentlemen, smitten by her Frenchness which—like flirting—she practised reflexively, having long ago cultivated the art of being 'French'. Her mother's only surviving friend, a saintly old woman named Wendy O'Brien, visited Marie in order to be lectured about everything she was doing wrong. To Marie, other people existed simply to cause her grief and interfere with her plans; she was constitutionally unable to see another person's point of view. Her mother—who had an uncanny ability to scramble other people's brains—also had a genius for alienating everyone.

Penny was thinking about Marie and did not notice tall, gangly Jonathan Lott, trailed by Bites, moving towards her from the opposite direction. By the time she noticed him she barely had time to pull in her stomach, which must have been sticking out, the wind flattening the T-shirt against her belly which, mercifully, was always slightly smaller in the mornings. 'Morning,' she said and Jonathan smiled. Bites wagged her tail.

She knew him, of course. Penny had been to several parties with Jonathan and Sarah, an intelligent woman with an engaging smile whom she remembered mostly for a truthful conversation they had once had about recalcitrant daughters. She knew Sarah had run off with a woman, a fact she found intensely interesting, but despite this she intended to give Jonathan only a friendly nod and keep walking.

'Penny!' he said, and she stopped and turned. 'I was going to drop in. I'm having a barbecue tonight, nothing fancy. Do you and PP want to join me? Gordie's coming, and the Pattersons and Rosanna.'

She laughed. 'You're forgetting Pete and I aren't married any more.'

He laughed too, a deep, sexy laugh. 'Oh, I thought you had one of those civilised divorces where you all go away on holiday together like in an Alan Alda movie.'

'Yeah, right,' she said.

Something of her feelings must have shown on her face, because Jonathan averted his eyes. 'Look, a kite,' he said.

She followed the line of his finger and saw a hawk, free-wheeling in the air. 'Oh, you mean a bird kite, not a kite kite.'

He laughed again. 'It's too early for those kites,' he said.

They both noticed, at the same time, the dog, eating a bright orange patch of vomit. 'She loves vomit,' said Penny.

'Doesn't everyone?' he said. Penny smiled.

'What time do you want me?' she said.

'Any time after seven,' he said.

'Okay,' she said. 'Oh, and what can I bring?' The polite response to this was 'nothing', and she was surprised when Jonathan suggested she could bring something sweet if she liked. What a tight-arse, she thought as they parted, asking people to dinner and then asking them to bring the dinner. According to gossip he was mean with his money, even though he had piles of it. He never gave mates rates on his house either: Phil's sixtieth birthday relatives had come from New Zealand and when Sylv asked Jonathan about the possibility of them staying at his house—assuming he would invite them to stay for free, or at the very least at a modest rental since it was empty—he let her know via Cheryl—via Cheryl, not even personally!—that, yes, it was available, but at the full price of comparable high-season rentals. Cheryl ran The Landing's only letting agency, and everyone knew that she had once had a one-night stand with Jonathan, but no-one knew the details. Everyone wanted to know, naturally.

FIVE

Marie Arene

In 1955, Penny's father, Syd, proposed to her mother, Marie, on Brisbane's Victoria Bridge. The sun was at last giving up its hold on another insufferably humid summer day and in the wet subtropical air Marie's new blue crepe de chine dress was sticking to her back. When she refused him, Syd turned around, climbed to the very top of the elaborately curved iron guard rails, and jumped into the Brisbane River.

Penny's mother watched the whole thing, her comprehension a beat behind what her eyes were telling her. She saw him climbing but, as in many other moments in life, she failed to predict one of the many infinite and impossible responses from another living being's veiled heart. Only when she heard the terrible sound of Syd's body hitting the water did she run for help.

Soon, boats were scouring the river and Marie was wringing her hands. How could she have known that the skinny youth with a crooked eye tooth held in his heart such outsized passions? Marie kept her own heart under lock and key, only rarely looking up to see the wash of marbled clouds over fathomless skies, causing her to puzzle afresh about why she stood on the earth at this particular spot at this particular time. Marie knew nothing good ever came of clouds momentarily parting or of trying to predict an outcome.

'What's his address, love?' said the policeman standing by her side with a notebook.

'I don't know,' she said. Marie did not like this turn of events and she knew her face was gathering itself in, even more so than usual. Marie did not like anyone knowing anything about her.

'There, there,' said the policeman, misreading her. 'It's not your fault, dear.' He made a move as if to comfort her and Marie pulled away.

As if it were her fault! What an idiotic man. Marie hated Australians for their stupidity and their smug complacency, and standing on the bridge on a ridiculously hot February evening she hated them all over again. She hated Brisbane with its small-town manners and its small-town bigwigs, and she hated the humid days and humid nights and the night cart and the nightman, the tin can resting on one shoulder, a man who spent his life emptying toilets of excrement, reeking and foul, crawling with maggots, abuzz with flies. It was like Africa! It was unimaginably awful, an uncivilised shanty town in which she was stranded without hope of return. She hated the wooden houses squatting on poles, the tin roofs, the chicken coops at the back of houses, the rows of outboxes in the awful treeless clipped backyards and the slimy frog who lived in the tin toilet. She hated the cheery signs by the side of the road reading *Stay Alive in '55* because every time she saw one a voice in her head instinctively replied, *I'd rather be dead*. She hated the witless policeman standing in front of her in an excited swoon of self-importance (how people who slept safe in their own beds loved catastrophe: death! suicide! drama!). She hated everything about the particular spot of the world she stood in, this land where nothing happened. Now something had happened but Marie still hated everything: everything, that was, except for poor, drowned Syd McAlister and his last violent, non-complacent act of defiant life.

But Syd wasn't drowned, obviously, since he went on to become Penny's father. When he hit the water he sank fast, but he must have chanced upon a deep part of the river. He felt the shock of the impact, but no worse than a bad belly flop, a painful stinging up through his legs and, strangely, all around his chin. His jaw must have slammed up against the top of his skull and for a moment he wondered if he had broken his teeth. He was thinking this as he rose, alive, to the surface, his tongue sliding fast around his mouth, numbering the molars and incisors still miraculously fixed in his head, thinking of being alive and breathing and still in love. He was thinking about Marie's dark, lovely face, as fine-boned as his mother's best teacups. He was thinking of those teacups, fine china, Royal Doulton, stacked in the mirrored china cabinet, the best china and the best china cabinet from his father's illustrious shop, McAlisters Department Store, the best shop in Fortitude

Valley. The bones of Marie's French face were like those fine china teacups, her skin burnished, darkly golden, unlike any other girl's, her eyes such a deep shade of brown they might be black. Teacups and bones, dark eyes, Marie and breath, swimming, swimming, the Churchie under-seventeen freestyle and breaststroke champion. Syd McAlister, exhilarated, with a full set of teeth, happier and more powerful than any other death-defying twenty-three-year-old in Brisbane. *Marie Arene, Marie Arene, Marie Arene*, the strange lovely notes of her name falling like a song upon his tongue.

He kept swimming. It seemed to him that his entire life had been aimed at this one moment, and that everything inside him had risen to this one exquisite point. He knew himself to be unlike timid men, destined to live their lives within the boundaries of propriety. His was to be a life ablaze, a life risked, gambled on the outcome of love. The tide was coming in, sweeping in from Moreton Bay, but Syd pushed against it. He swam hard, past a barge, past the cliffs at Kangaroo Point, and up and under the giant span of the Story Bridge. He was invincible, powering past the docks with its ships, past safe men just coming on nightshift, their lunchboxes packed for smoko. He swam on and on, marvelling at how love had not killed him and how impending death had not killed love. He swam around the bend in the river, *Marie Arene, Marie Arene*, till at last he came upon the baths at Mowbray Park. It was growing dark and the water was murky because there had been a lot of rain. He battled his way past logs and branches, over the pebbled rim of the baths, and it was only as he was climbing up the stone steps to the river bank that he realised he was buggered. He looked down at his body in the twilight and saw that dark bruises were forming on his chest. His shirt! He had lost his best shirt, without knowing it, and saw for the first time that he was wearing only trousers, socks and one shoe.

He shook himself down, and headed up the hill across the park. The Moreton Bay figs formed an archway, dim and shivering, as he crossed the footpath. A sort of porous membrane between life and death had opened, between the natural and the supernatural, between the material world and the unseen world, which he had experienced only once before. He was unclear what this new unseen world revealed; only that its perceptive reach had been uncovered, and that he was imbued with the same reverential ringing feeling that had filled him when his father died, long after the nurses had given him up for dead, long after Dr Gregg said that his father could no longer hear them. 'Hearing is the last of the senses to go,' Dr Gregg said. 'I fear Alan is no longer with us.' Not long after this, Syd's father had squeezed his hand. At the point of death—after struggling for some hours, the rattle in his throat sounding exactly like something Syd had heard before in dreams, a rattle that really was a death rattle—his father squeezed his hand. The colour drained from him at the moment of his extinction, his flesh no longer animated by moving blood but turned to wax. Syd walked from the room, the permeable membrane rent, to find the world as he had never known it: tender, perishing, awash with souls.

Syd felt the same way as he climbed from the river. He was alive, walking, in love with Marie Arene, a resurrected man. When he got to his front door, a policeman opened it. His mother, Min, stood behind the policeman who had just finished telling her that Syd had drowned.

'Hello, Mum,' Syd said.

His mother fainted.

SIX

The art of life

Around three the phone rang. Penny was asleep, book on happiness—another volume to add to the enormous library she had accrued in her ceaseless quest for instruction in the art of life—squashed under her thigh. She was momentarily discombobulated, unsure where the ringing was coming from. By the time she got to the phone, whoever it was had hung up, but they had left a message. *'It's Gloria from Evergreen Gardens. Can you please call me urgently?'* Penny's heart gave a little flip: here was the moment, arrived. Her mouth went dry and her legs felt weak; with one hand she pulled across the nearest chair. The nursing home number was stored in the phone, thank God, and she pressed the button. It went straight through to Gloria's answer phone, so she rang the general line. 'Gloria's looking for me,' she said. 'Is my mother all right?' The dopey girl immediately went into the I'm-sorry-I'm-not-authorised spiel, which Penny assumed to mean her mother was dead. Oh, God, she thought, no, no, please. All the wrecked moments between them crowded in, all the missed chances, the right words unsaid. The hammering in her head and heart was so loud she almost failed to hear a voice on the other end of the phone. 'Mrs Collins? Mrs Collins?' The voice cut through the noise that had engulfed her. 'Mrs Collins? Are you there?' When she finally heard it, the voice was saying that her mother was alive and well (apart from an eye infection), but could no longer live at Evergreen Gardens.

Penny knew, of course, how difficult Marie was. She knew about the ordering around, the rudeness, the nurses who refused to help her following her recent fall, who did not wish to shuffle her into the shower cubicle to sit her on a white plastic seat to be handwashed like a prestige car. She knew about the indiscriminate flirting, her mother's vain insistence that she was the most attractive woman her age in any room she was in; how she thoughtlessly insulted every other woman by implying that, because she was French, she genetically had a better fashion sense than they did. She knew about Marie's complaints regarding the food, the disappointing company, the service in general. The service was nothing like what she was used to, nothing like the five-star hospital she had once stayed in when she twisted her ankle in Paris on that last wonderful trip with Syd, when every evening she was offered a *carte du jour* featuring crustaceans or the meats of hand-reared beasts, a Kir Royale to drink while she decided. Australians did not know how to do anything properly! She was indestructible; a vigorous eighty-eight years old with all her wits, and she had outwitted everyone.

Penny had a younger sister, Rosemary, who lived a charmed life on the other side of Australia. 'One can never live too far away from one's mother,' Rosemary said with boring frequency. Rosemary had a devoted husband and a son who did all the right things, who ate his greens and went to university and—unlike Scarlett—never ran off with anyone inappropriate. Penny had flown to Perth with Marie for his wedding, at great expense, and everything was in its rightful place: the church, the groom, the bride, the guests. No-one got drunk, the speeches were on the right side of bawdy, and Penny hated every minute of it. She couldn't work out why some people's lives went in exactly the right direction, all their lives long; they married the right person at the right age, had the right children at the right age, and their children did everything expected of them. The right children did not run off with men old enough to be their fathers, birth two babies in quick succession and fail to qualify as anything other than an unskilled worker. Other people had handsome, successful husbands who flew them to Italy to eat expensive sardines by the sea at Portofino. Other people made great paintings, like Lucian Freud, instead of living with the ghost of the person they might have been. Penny lived with a smothered self, someone shinier, braver and altogether more glorious.

'I'm really sorry but I'm in the middle of a conference,' Rosemary said now. 'I've been planning it all year. I can't possibly have her.' Rosemary was in marketing, whatever that was.

'But I had her last time,' Penny said, conscious that they were somehow playing out their childhood roles, with Penny always coveting something Rosemary had, and Rosemary refusing to relinquish the coveted object. Neither of them coveted Marie. She was conscious of a note of pleading in her voice. The last time Marie was dismissed from a nursing home had been right in the midst of the scandal of Scarlett and Paul Raymond, with Marie in the spare room shouting at Penny that her mother, Penny's unknown, tragic grandmother, was married and pregnant at eighteen, so what was the problem? 'Their bodies are made for it,' Marie said in her maddeningly distinctive accent, the French language still curling around her English words, three-quarters of a century—more—after she'd left her native country.

'People died at thirty in the Middle Ages, too, Marie. How does that have anything to do with anything in the twenty-first century?' Penny shouted back down the hall.

'Girls and boys still have the same bodies, Middle Ages, twenty-first century,' said Marie.

'Christ, will you shut up!' Penny said, too loudly, and her mother would not speak to her for the rest of the time it took to get her settled in a new nursing home.

'I've got to pick her up,' she said to Rosie. 'Pronto.'

'Can't you put her in a cab and send her to a hotel? Russ and I will pay.'

Penny had thought of this herself, but could not bear to do that to her mother. There was nothing for it: she would have to bring Marie home.

Who knew that residents could even be rejected from nursing homes? And this time Penny had been so careful about reading the fine print! Her late father, Syd, had inherited a small fortune in McAlisters Department Store, a once-grand shop modelled on Liberty of London, situated in what was then one of the smartest shopping areas of Brisbane, Fortitude Valley. For many years McAlisters was *the* store to go to in provincial

Brisbane, to be fitted for bespoke dresses and suits, to purchase wedding trousseaux, ladies' stockings, gifts, the best-quality household linen; it was where young couples went to lay-by furniture for their newly built houses. During the store's heyday in the fifties and sixties, Marie and Syd went on six-week tours of the Continent every northern summer, and every Australian summer they rented apartments in Surfers Paradise opposite the beach, at Kinkabool or The Chevron, where they hosted lavish cocktail parties in the Corroboree Room, attended by all the big shots: the lord mayors of Brisbane and the Gold Coast, venal police commissioners, consecutive newspaper editors, High Court judges, various premiers and high-ranking public servants who with giddy abandon appointed sons, daughters, nephews, friends or anyone they liked the look of, because nepotism—not to mention institutionalised corruption—was the order of the day. Anyone who was anyone came to the McAlisters' specially catered parties to make small talk and hear all the gossip, while eating devils-on-horseback, smoked oysters and gherkins smothered in cream cheese and swaddled in a processed meat product called devon, served by tanned young women in gold lamé bikinis.

Even today Marie was rich—she owned several buildings in Brisbane's CBD—and had enough money to go into any nursing home she liked. Marie did not yet appreciate that the question was no longer which nursing home she liked, but which nursing home liked her.

During the long drive back to The Landing, Marie issued a constant stream of directions.

'It is shorter turning off the next exit,' she said. 'Your father always drove up past Cooroy.'

Yeah, and this highway wasn't even built when he died, Penny replied in her head. She was getting a sharp pain in the left side of her skull.

If Penny ever wondered why she could not bring herself to hug her mother or tell her that she loved her, she remembered her decision at eighteen to stop calling her 'Mum' and to address her forever after as 'Marie'. It seemed to Penny the only way she could distinguish her mother from herself, to know that her body was not her mother's body. She could not breathe properly around Marie; their relationship had a claustrophobic intensity, in that Marie had powerfully and mysteriously conveyed to Penny her obligation to fulfil her dreams and assuage her fears. Her mother's life was built on the ruins of loss: the suicide of her mother, her only brother killed in the war, her father's premature death. She had once been a girl living in an elegant apartment in the sixteenth arrondissement, in Passy, with a maid and an English tutor. Now Marie was alone, a permanent citizen of some invisible city under siege, and Penny, helpless, tried to signal she was outside its gates. She conceded that her strategy of refusing to name her mother had not altered her mother's perception of Penny as an extension of herself. Penny knew all this and could not understand how her vast self-knowledge had failed to change for the better a single thing in her life.

At last, after driving for what seemed like hours, Penny swung the car into her driveway at The Landing. She got out and walked around to the passenger side to open the door for her mother.

'You are too fat around the middle, Penny,' Marie said. 'You should diet.'

Penny paused, looking down at her mother, not yet willing to help her up. Unlike every other old woman, Marie wore her silver hair long, swept up behind her head in an elegant roll.

'What? Is the truth a crime?' said Marie. 'Truth gives a short answer, lies go the long way. Penny, I am your mother. You are too fat.'

SEVEN

A dazzled world

Hippolyte, a fruit of love, a cherub of a baby boy who might have stepped straight from a Baroque trompe-l'oeil ceiling, was sleeping on his back. One plump fist rested against his juicy face, his cheeks slightly inflamed because he was teething. Blond curls lay damp across his forehead, the curls Scarlett refused to cut, even though everyone took him for a girl. His lips—his lips!—so ripe, so glossy, so swollen, more beautiful than any photoshopped model. He was delicious, lustrous, and Scarlett could eat him, except that eating Hippolyte would wake him up.

Scarlett stood on one leg, looking down into her baby son's cot, her eldest son stirring in his new bed on the opposite side of the room. Ajax was proudly sleeping in his first grown-up bed, fashioned like a racing car; a bed Paul had ordered especially. Paul had put it up himself, too, the kids jumping all over him, and he had never once lost his temper. Afternoon nap time was Scarlett's favourite, the only moment she felt halfway competent as a mother. She loved to gaze at her children's sleeping faces—fed, alive, unbroken—astonished that she, Scarlett, could be responsible for a human life, and not just one life but two, keeping them safe from fire, water, snakes, poison. She was not a very good mother, she knew; she could not stop them fighting, knocking each other senseless or else screaming their heads off. Once, when Ajax was not yet walking, she had lifted him into a tree beside the lake, carefully wedging his fat nappied bottom into the fork of two branches so that he resembled a plump koala, stepping back to take a photograph at precisely the same moment he fell headfirst to the ground. There was an awful second of silence before he erupted into a mighty howl; the particular silence that told her it was going to be bad, that he was gathering every ounce of outrage and pain, and that it was going to require yet another call to her mother and a race into Gympie Hospital. Ajax's lip was split, and there was a nasty cut above his eye, but mercifully no bone was broken. There was so much blood that at first Scarlett was sure she had killed him, that the blood sealed inside his skin had broken free, and was destined to flow till it ran out.

'You put him in a tree?' Paul said. 'A baby who can barely sit up?'

She could not explain how she thought she had thoroughly calculated the risk, nor how she had so spectacularly miscalculated it. That night she cried and cried in Paul's arms, and it was not until the early hours of the morning, Paul's mouth upon the soft rise between her legs, her orgasm bursting upon his poetic tongue, that she knew Ajax was going to be all right, that she and Paul were going to be all right, that whatever strange, ravishing terrors were upon them, they had between them forever and ever this stupendous glory, unspooling, a dazzled world.

She heard Paul's car, the engine, his, the sound she could hear from a thousand kilometres away, distinguishing it from all the other engines, as a new mother distinguishes her own baby's cry from every other baby's. Paul! Her lover, her man, and, very soon, her very own husband.

Scarlett was waiting in the yard as Paul drove in. The sight of him still caused her stomach to leap: the curve of his neck, the big, manly bullish chest. She loved his smell; the hair on his chest; the precise shape and feel of his balls and cock. Two children, almost five years since he first lifted her skirt and placed his fingers gently at her centre, causing her heart to go flying up, up, up from her body, flung out, not only to him but beyond him, to that place where love lived, wild, holy. If Scarlett's fine beauty ran straight down from Marie through the maternal line, her heart was her grandfather Syd's, destined to make large and inappropriate claims on love, to stake everything she had on a blazing moment. Not for her the crimped life of her mother, the downturned mouth, the might-have-beens, the slow leak of everyday tedium. Scarlett was going down in flames, Scarlett was burning, Scarlett was going to turn her mother's life on its head, and her father's, and set the tongues of The Landing wagging so hard they might be in danger of breaking off from their stalks.

'What are you doing home, babe?' she asked, running up and flinging herself into her lover's arms.

'Can't a man take an early mark if he wants to?' Paul had a temporary contract with a small, crappy IT company on the coast, but he was looking for better work.

'Come on, quick,' she said. 'The boys are asleep.'

And Scarlett took Paul's hand and led him inside, where they lay upon their double bed, breathing into one another's grateful mouths, the air alive and ringing with birdsong.

EIGHT

Pants man

Dr Gordon 'Gordie' Wallace, GP, retired, saw the lucky back of Paul Raymond being led inside by temptation. From his window opposite, he watched Scarlett lightly tripping along the grass, barefoot, beautiful, her hair tangled. She was just the sort of girl he would have fallen for too, back in the day when he was a pants man. Gordie's late wife, Pam, had turned a blind eye to his shenanigans throughout their happy marriage of forty-nine years (she died of bowel cancer, nastily, a year off their fiftieth wedding anniversary), only ever making a single reference to his philandering. Gordie remembered it clearly: they had been at lunch at the Orpheus, in those fine, hopeful days before she got ill, when they were in the process of selling their house in Melbourne's Malvern East and looking around for somewhere at The Landing to rent until they could buy. Gordie was enjoying the slender form of the wee Asian lassie who had just served them their drinks, watching her shapely little arse as she walked off.

'I should get you a new business card, darling,' Pam said. *'Gordon Wallace, Pants Man, Retired.'*

He looked at her, astonished, but Pammy was smiling, her kind eyes crinkling in her much-loved old face.

Before Malvern East, and before that, Kew, Gordie had run a medical practice with Pam working as his receptionist in a small town in the Scottish Borders. Gordie was a brilliant working-class boy from Glasgow, whose mind was lit up by an English master with a love of the poetry of Robbie Burns. Gordie caught poetry like an infection, Burns and Yeats and the long-abandoned poetry of the poet and soldier Sir Walter Raleigh; Latin, the poetry of Virgil, the long, mesmeric incantations to everything marvellous; the poetry learned by heart, reading his eyes out, deep into the cold Scottish nights. His family had worked the docks for generations and did not know what to do with a lad who was dux of his grammar school and then won a scholarship to study medicine at the University of Glasgow. He was the only remaining boy of the family, the other two having perished from pneumonia; in the 1940s, and for a decade after, Scotland had the highest child death rates of anywhere in Ireland and the United Kingdom. The way the working class lived was positively medieval, and some nights during his early years of training, Gordie broke down and sobbed. It was into Pam's bonny bosom he sobbed. Pam, the pretty Australian nurse from the children's ward at Glasgow Hospital, Pammy with the dimple in one cheek and masses of curling strawberry blonde hair. He did not know what strawberry blonde hair was until he saw Pam's: golden, white, rippling, shot through with the faintest blush of orange, tumbling down from her shoulders when he took the pins out.

They already had Anna when they migrated to Australia, and Pam was pregnant with James. Simon was born in Australia too, his poor scoundrel second son, who Gordie hadn't seen for a decade. Marijuana, amphetamines—and not, he hoped, heroin—whatever drug was going in Melbourne in the 1970s, Simon took it. Sometimes Gordie comforted himself with the thought that it was genetic: his father was a drunk, and his grandfather. But sad, sweet-tempered Pammy never got over it and Simon never got over his grief at his mother's death.

Gordie would never have left her. He put his sexual indiscretions in a separate box to that in which Pam and the children lived. No woman was ever Pam's equal, no woman as sweet, no woman knew him inside and out, backwards and front. His passing fancies were just that, passing, a sort of twitch, some fatal weakness that came from growing up Presbyterian, church every Sunday, eyes front, the long remorseless line of dockside workers behind him, bearing down. He had broken free, rejecting everything he might have been but not only that; rejecting everything that had made him. He had leaped a class in a single bound and for a while Gordie reckoned he deserved a mistress, in the same way he deserved his success, his comfortable middle-class house, his standing in the community, the exclusive private schools for the children. He might even have supposed himself French and not working-class Scots, lying back on expensive sheets in hotels on afternoons while the rest of the world was at work, his current mistress pouring him a drink, as in a sophisticated Continental movie.

He regretted it now. He regretted being eighty-six years old, a widower who drank too much in order to pass the time on wind-fuelled lonely evenings. He regretted mistaking the drink, the girl, the hotel room for something it was not. It was not an adventure in which he played the lead role but his actual life being lived, his future being cast, his character under construction. Now he would prefer to look back on his long life and find it blameless. Now that his ability to act on desire had fled (his last, final humiliating attempt was ten years before, with a comely young widow of sixty-six—unfortunately also the best friend of Phyllis from the shop—who had sucked and stroked his reluctant member before unceremoniously giving up and marching straight down to Phyllis and Phil and Sylv at the shop to announce he was a dud in the sack. At least that was how Gordie remembered it: the news of his failure broadcast by Radio Sylvia within minutes of his disgrace). Sex was everything, and nothing.

Now Gordie wished for those minutes back, the hours, so that he might lay them at Pam's feet. *The flowers do fade,* as the poet said; *fancy's spring, but sorrow's fall,* he might have said, too, if he could remember the lines, while at the same time an image passed through his head of Scarlett Collins's slender waist, leading into temptation. He feared that if he had those hours back again he might once again follow his mistakes; that his character was already set, irretrievably flawed. He wished he were a better man but he knew that he was not.

He saw Bites coming down the road, a what-fun-is-about-to-happen-now look on her face. He was inordinately attached to the stupid wee creature, the only living thing in the entire world who was entranced by him, as if every single time she laid eyes on him she could not believe her luck. She trailed him everywhere, except when she was not off like a Glasgow bint, following other men. She was a darling, his darling, and he moved away from the window to the front door and called her. Hearing his voice, everything in her sprang to attention: her tail, her ears, her head, her legs, bringing her bounding towards him, covered in love. If dogs could smile, and Gordie was very sure Bites could, she was not only smiling but grinning from ear to ear. Her favourite person in the whole wide world, him, Gordie Wallace, pants man, retired.

Gordie was concentrating on Bites and hadn't seen Jonathan bringing up the rear. Jonathan had been into Cooroy, to the butcher shop, to buy good rump steak and fresh organic beef sausages, and had just put them in the fridge when he decided that rather than ring old Gordie, he would wander up and ask him in person. He was fairly sure that even though the invitation was a late one, Gordie would be free. Jonathan prided himself on turning on a decent barbecue and was fond of the irregular social occasions held on the enormous back deck flowing out from his house. He fancied himself a social sort of man, a joiner, an active—and useful—member of society. Sarah liked to portray him as awkward or socially clumsy, when he considered himself socially adept. 'Making smart-arse comments is not my idea of witty repartee,' she once said. He reasoned that men and women had different ideas about humour, about friendship, about love—about everything, really, now that he thought about it. He was hardly friendless; not for him city manners of minding your own business and a preference for keeping neighbours at a respectful, safe distance. Jonathan had no truck with Brisbane people who owned houses at The Landing but who never joined in.

'Comrade! Grand to see ye!' said Gordie in curly Glaswegian, clinging, still, to his tongue. Gordie sometimes turned it up a notch but he could not retreat the other way, to the flat, featureless plains of the Australian accent. He was always surprised on his irregular trips home to see his remaining sister, Nene, that she thought he sounded Australian.

'How are you, my friend?' Jonathan said, loping over, ducking his head shyly. No wonder the ladies fancy him, Gordie thought, as Jonathan enveloped him in a huge, affectionate Australian hug. Gordie could not get over how personable Australians generally were. On his trips to Brisbane to see some medical specialist or other (don't ask) he caught buses and trains and noted that people frequently said 'Morning!' or smiled at each other, often tossing a cheery 'Thank you, driver!' over their shoulders when getting off a bus. In certain parts of Glasgow, when he was growing up, you were in danger of getting glassed if you looked sideways at someone.

'Well, I woke up this morning—that's something,' Gordie said. 'Getting old's better than the other thing.' By nature a convivial man, he immediately perked up. Being in the company of other souls was excellent for mental health.

'Do ye feel like a wee dram?' he said. 'I've an excellent Burgundy, just cracked.'

'Too early for me I'm afraid,' Jonathan said, suspicious, as ever, of Gordie's improbable, pantomime accent. 'Oh, go on, why not? Sun's over the yardarm,' he added, out of kindness.

Gordie was already on his way to his filthy kitchen, where plates of half-eaten food lay about, strung with insects. Piles of encrusted dishes were piled up, various tins and bottles. Jonathan regretted saying yes, but what disease could you possibly catch drinking from a dirty glass? He had never met Gordie's late wife, Pam, long dead before Jonathan got to know him, but he didn't doubt they had one of those marriages in which the duties of life were strictly divided along gender lines. Not for the first time he wondered if his own marriage might have fared better if Sarah had been one of those women who stayed at home gently tending the hearth, instead of dropping the girls at childcare and going off to become a high-ranking health department bureaucrat. On certain afternoons, leaving the office, he had longed for Sarah to be waiting at the end of the road, a bright, steady fixture, permanent as stars. If, these days, the stars were no longer steady, nor the earth itself assured, what hope was there for love? What was love but the frailest rope, thrown out to infinity, cast off into nothingness? Jonathan looked around the slovenly room, shorn of a woman, shorn of the warm, organising hand that belonged to Sarah and all the other women who had shepherded and shaped male life, starting with his mother. He had no answers.

He took the glass, which was oily.

'*Santé*,' said Gordie, knocking it back as if it were water.

Jonathan took a sip. It was surprisingly open, velvety, warm in the throat.

'Good, isn't it,' said Gordie. It was not a question. 'From my old mate Trevor's cellar. Twelve years old.'

'Excellent,' Jonathan said. 'Now what have you been up to, you old scoundrel?'

'Oh, you know, continuing my valiant search for a wealthy widow with a bad cough,' he said.

Bites, who had been standing between them wagging her tail, torn between two lovers, suddenly rushed off to the front door, barking uproariously. A woman walked in, a small, pretty woman in a pair of skimpy shorts and an unbuttoned shirt revealing overflowing breasts. Jonathan took her in—two seconds, three—his eyes travelling quickly to her face.

'Anna!' Gordie said. 'My God! What are you doing here?'

'Hello, Pa,' she said. 'It wasn't locked.' No-one locked their houses at The Landing, not even after a small band of teenage thieves from Gympie was found to be regularly knocking over empty holiday homes.

'Charles has left me,' she said. 'I had nowhere to go.'

'Sweetheart!' said Gordie, opening his arms. 'Why didn't you call? When did you fly in? Is Gaspard with you?'

'It's term time,' she said. 'He's still in school. Oh, Pa, I'm exhausted, that trip is a nightmare. And then I had to drive all that way from the airport. I only stopped to change my clothes.'

Where had she come from? Jonathan wondered. *Gaspard*?

'Darling, I have a guest,' said Gordie, letting her go and turning to face him. 'Anna, this is my dear neighbour Jonathan. May I introduce my daughter, who appears to have lost her husband? She's had four already. The next one's bound to be the right one.' He winked at Jonathan over his daughter's skinny shoulders.

'It's not a joke, Pa!' said Anna, beginning to cry. 'I feel as if I'm dying of sadness.'

'Aye, darlin', I know, I know,' said Gordie in his terrible, corny accent.

As he walked home, Jonathan had a picture in his head of Anna's slim back, the full breasts on the elegant frame. He was conscious, too, of a great rope of hair snaking down her back like Rapunzel's, but dark, not golden. She had just flown all the way from London, which—as far as fleeing wrecked marriages goes—was as dramatic a gesture as you could get. Why hadn't she gone to a friend or a nearby hotel? Clearly she was not that sort of woman. She had a son at a posh boarding school somewhere, Winchester or Westminster, not quite Eton, but one of those schools in which the British ruling class perpetuates its rights of succession. Four husbands! How could anyone man up a second time, let alone a third and a fourth? Jonathan's heart recoiled from love as if from a striking snake; his once fulsome heart cowered in his chest. He recalled one of the last exchanges he'd had with Sarah, just before she left to set up house with Cath; he had been away, in Cairns, and he sent what he thought was an affectionate email, telling her of everything he had been doing. He signed off *fondest regards*, and it was this she had flung back in his face. 'Fondest regards? Who signs off an email to their wife *fondest regards*? You are unbelievable!' She said he was tone deaf when it came to love and, furthermore, he no idea what intimacy was. 'Who are you, Jonathan? What moves you? What scares you? I have no idea.' Of course she knew who he was! She was being

51

ridiculous, yet everything she said struck him like an arrow: he had a sensation of being under physical bombardment, as if cowering from attack. He loved her! If the right words for love were dumb on his tongue, his love was everywhere manifest, in the life they had built together, in the children they had made. How had he failed to notice the moment when emotive womanly feelings became the benchmark of everything good, replacing the restrained, chin-up blokeish moral code he had grown up with? Now, men like him who had failed to become feminised males were regarded with suspicion, considered buttoned-up, secretive, *repressed*. Surely Sarah knew that everyone was filled—to an astonishing degree—with what they could never say? What words could ever possibly hope to speak the dimensions of love? He didn't know what Sarah wanted, not really; what she wanted him to do, what she wanted him to say or to be. How had he failed to notice how unhappy she must have been?

Walking along, his head down, he was suddenly overwhelmed by the endless exercises demanded by love, its interminable arm-wrestling. He was overcome by pity, a great unending pool of useless pity, for himself, for Sarah, for Anna, for old Gordie, for every man and woman who had ever tried to master love and failed.

He had experienced erotic adventures since Sarah's departure, of course, many of them happy; he could still conjure in his mind's eye the gleaming haunches of the young black woman from Nigeria straddling him, joyfully drawing his orgasm from him. He remembered Donna, hot-headed young Donna, who for a time he believed he might love, until he recognised that she did not care for intellectual debate or, like him, see life as a test of courage. Donna had no capacity for commiseration.

To distract himself from memory he went through the ever-expanding list of barbecue guests as he walked: Rosanna; Penny, and now her mother, Marie, who had apparently turned up like a bad penny; Gordie and his attractive daughter, Anna; that miserable bastard PP, ex-husband of Penny, and Cheryl from the rental agency, who PP shared a house with; and Glen and Celia Quinn, his immediate neighbours. That made ten, counting him. He hadn't asked Penny's daughter, Scarlett, and Paul Raymond, but maybe he should have. He walked on, faster. He had thirty or even forty years left to him; he had plenty of time, and yet he felt as if time were running out. Two years since Sarah left, more; he was practically divorced! Enough, mate, enough.

PART

II

NINE

Banishment

On a hot Brisbane night in February 1955, Marie made her way home, accompanied by two overexcited policemen. The first policeman, the one from the bridge, kept swivelling around in the front seat of the police car, asking her questions.

'How're you liking Australia, dear? I bet Brisbane's a nice change, eh? The place is looking pretty spruce these days.'

She refused to talk to him. She had just watched a man jump to his death. She stood unveiled, exposed, contaminated once more by the imprint of death. She could not halt the throb of grief; her teeth had set up a shivering in her skull, as if it were cold, cold, cold, like the dismal nights in London she endured without heat, that perishing flat in a bad street in Primrose Hill, the eerie lines of the bombed house next door through the bedroom window, as if it were still cold and she was not now sticking to the upholstery, miserably hot. Was there to be no escape?

How did she even end up in Australia? She should have gone to Canada instead of being beguilded by Wendy McCann's romantic nonsense about Brisbane. How random her existence, how haphazard! She had once had a mother and a father and a brother named Eric—an entire life. She had once been her father's favourite, sitting on a high stool in his warm office watching him work, her kind moustachioed father, a prosperous manufacturer of leather goods, her mother unfit for anything, forever locking herself in the bathroom and threatening to kill herself or else packing her bags, screaming that she was leaving, because she was so unloved in her own home. Marie had once been thirteen years old, begging her father to let her go to boarding school in England not because she wanted to benefit from an English education, as she told him, but because her mother was cruel, depressed and overly dramatic. And while Marie was in England the war began and her old life disappeared, *pouf*: the elegant apartment, the hysterical mother, the kindly father, the brother named Eric—the miserable family dynamics—all of it, gone.

'Your English is very good, dear,' the policeman said. 'Bonza, as we say in Brisso.'

'My English is superior to yours,' she said. 'Australian is barely even English.' She hated him. Would he never stop talking? She kept her eyes turned to the window.

'Well, excuse me, Lady Muck.'

The other policeman, the one driving, tried to shush his colleague. 'For Pete's sake, lay off. She's in shock.'

Marie had tried to tell him that she did not require assistance and, in particular, she most especially did not want to arrive home in a police car. She had attempted to march off but the chatterbox policeman restrained her by the arm as if she were under arrest. All the questions, all the questions, the throb in her chest, the hand on her arm, she was being marshalled, questioned, sitting in her English class, fifteen years old, an elderly, red-faced policeman arriving at the classroom door. Could she please accompany him to the headmistress's office? Her heart stopped, every eye upon her, her hands sweated, she did not want to go to the headmistress's office to be told whatever dreadful thing she was going to be told. Trembling, Marie said *yes, yes*, to the policeman asking her questions now, agreed to accompany him to a police car to shut him up, to stop him asking questions, to prevent attracting even more attention to herself than she already had. She longed to disappear into the crowd, to be indistinguishable, the same as the rest, not singular, picked out by her losses. She was not grateful.

Of course everyone came rushing from the house as soon as the police car drew up. Mrs McCann, Mr McCann—clearly in the midst of his tea, a napkin fluttering from the collar of his shirt—Wendy McCann, Terry McCann, with his withered polio leg, and Lance McCann, who had recently been in hospital with the gastric.

'Oh, dear God, what has happened?' Mrs McCann cried.

'Mother! Language!' said Mr McCann, unaccustomed to hearing his wife take the Lord's name in vain. The McCanns were Catholics, with many more children absent from the house, but still willing to drive Marie to the hot wooden box that was All Saints' Church of England, Chermside, every Sunday. The McCanns, tumbling down the front stairs of the wooden house on wooden posts, twelve feet in the air, spilling onto the treeless expanse of their front lawn, flinging up their hands. Not a tree in sight! Nothing, not a leaf, not a branch, not a flower, not a skerrick of blessed leafy relief from the humid air, thick and wet and smothering as the festering air of Asia, from the blast of the antipodean sun boiling in the sky, a great, molten, unblinking eye, glaring down. Roasted alive she was, sweating in her skin, day after merciless day.

Marie stepped now from the police car, shading her eyes against the glare coming off the house, still, the sun already retreated.

'A cup of tea,' said Mrs McCann. 'Wendy, a slice of seed-cake for the officers.'

'Yes, Mum,' said Wendy, scooting fast up the front stairs. Safe little Wendy McCann, with her matching luggage, her good set of pearls from FW Nissen and her rosary, once a teacher with Marie for the overcrowded classes at Princess Road Junior Mixed and Infants School, Primrose Hill, London. Marie, at the beginning of her long disappearance, eating almost nothing, barely sleeping, and Wendy, a shadowless Australian girl, who soon had the room of scared four-year-olds entranced by her story of what had happened when she was four years old, just like them, accidentally dropping something through the front stairs of a house far away, in Queensland, Australia, and getting her head stuck. 'What did you drop, Miss?' a grimy boy asked.

'Well, you know what,' said Wendy. 'I can't even remember! I think it might have been my dolly, but at any rate I was trying to get whatever it was that had fallen through, sticking my hand down first, and then my arm, and finally squeezing my head and shoulders between the steps. But then I couldn't pull my head out again!'

By now Marie, introducing Miss McCann to her new classroom, was listening as hard as the children. 'What happened, Miss? What happened?' the children said, shouting, laughing, leaping from their seats.

'Well, I called to my mother and our neighbour, who had become such a close friend of my mother's that we called her Aunty Bee. They were having a cup of tea in the kitchen and they rushed out to try to free me but, after several goes at trying to get me out, it was clear I was well and truly stuck. I was wedged right in.'

The children stared. 'Aunty Bee said, "I'll go and phone the fire brigade. They'll have to come and saw through the steps." Well, I don't know which of the words it was—"fire brigade" or "saw"—but my head came straight out, pop, just like that!'

And now here was Marie, delivered to her future in the Commonwealth of Australia via a free passage courtesy of the government. Australian citizens did not even exist before 1949—she would have been a British subject if she'd arrived before then—and here she was, reborn, an Australian citizen walking up the head-swallowing steps.

•

She did not see Syd McAlister that week, or the next. The news came that he was alive, direct from his sister, Evelyn McAlister, the grade five teacher with whom Marie taught at Chermy, Chermside State School. 'It's a miracle,' said Evelyn as they walked to the tram stop on Gympie Road. Seeing a tram coming, they made a run for it. The tram was open on both sides, and rain and wind blew in. 'Oh, my hair!' said Evelyn, reaching into her handbag for her scarf. Marie was not thinking of her hair but recalling the stumble of *yes* upon her tongue, of being the ruinous catalyst for Syd McAlister's terrible ascent.

She heard her daughter now, moving around the kitchen. She would buy Penny a copy of that new diet book she had read about, a diet supposedly followed by cavemen or at least by hunter-gatherers, men and women who feasted when they had food and fasted when they did not. Penny was a child of fortune, untested, a woman who spent too much of her time worrying about love. The thought of her daughter's good fortune did not make Marie happy, not exactly. Her thoughts drifted instead to a new idea, how she could easily convert the large garage area beneath Penny's house into a granny flat. She added *granny flat* to the words *diet book* in the large invisible ledger she kept in her brilliant, vigorous old head. The lump near her eye was getting bigger.

TEN

Radio Sylvia

Onions! He'd forgotten onions. Bad temper threatened for a moment but, as always, Jonathan remembered his foul-tempered father who made everyone's life a misery, so he took a deep breath and exhaled slowly through his mouth. His father, a suburban solicitor, found everything trying: a broken tap, tax returns, driving, children who failed to be anything other than children, forgotten onions. No matter, Jonathan thought, I'll nick down to the shop. He whipped off the apron featuring Escoffier's recipe for soufflé which Sarah had given him when he had been going through his French cooking phase. Men cooking was something Sarah approved of, one of the many things about him she liked: theirs was not a disharmonious marriage or one filled with strife. They rarely argued about the mechanics of daily life, or about anything else; he had supposed them to be living together companionably, affectionately, side by side, worn into each other like weathered rocks. He flung the apron on the bench.

Bites was waiting when he opened the door. 'You wee darling!' he said, trying to sound like Gordie. She leaped up. 'Come on, let's go and see Sylv.' He had no internet connection or mobile reception at the house, a radical thing, a deliberate choice to cast off into speechless space. He felt oddly disembodied, and reflexively picked up his mobile and put it in his back pocket, hopeful it might pick up a signal somewhere along the way. Occasionally his mobile inexplicably picked up reception, but it was unpredictable, random. He wasn't expecting anything in particular anyway but text messages, like email, had come to seem to him a modern cargo cult, in which unspecified good fortune might at any moment be delivered to him by supernatural forces. At work, he checked his emails as constantly as a teenage girl.

The wind had dropped and birdsong was sweeping the air, scented now with flowers from the two big old frangipani trees by the side of the road, rosy halos of flowers arranged like bouquets among its leaves. The light was going from the sky, which had a soft bruised quality; parakeets jewelled the trees, bright reds and greens, a flash of orange. Scrub turkeys rooted around in the undergrowth; a couple of bats swung overhead, the translucent cut of their dark wings outlined against the deepening early evening. Close by, bats in the trees squabbled, the thwack of their wings as loud as a wet dog shaking itself down, its ears slapping. The birds, the scrub turkeys, the noisy bats, the lake spread out before his eyes, the ruffle of the air contrived to soothe him as he walked: nature's grace, bestowed. Jonathan had once been a religious boy, his heart called to Jesus by a particularly beguiling priest at his Anglican boys' school, a charismatic, who blazed with the spirit of the wondrous God capable of seeing through walls and witnessing everything that a masturbating thirteen-year-old boy did in the privacy of his own bed. Jonathan hadn't been a believer for years, but he still had what he thought of as a deep streak of *religiosity*, a heart shaped for praising, a willingness to believe in the numinous cloud of unknowing.

Ahead, he saw a small girl drawing on the road in bright pink chalk. Straight away he knew it was the child, Giselle, who declared herself her *Giselleness* in the hopscotch drawing outside the new toilet block. Dare he say hello? It was so hard these days; cameras banned from school concerts and sports days because of paedophiles, or the fear of them. He still hadn't decided whether to say hello or not when the child looked up, startled, quickly gathered up her chalks and ran away.

He watched her scuttling through the bushes and into the dark backyard of one of Gordie's two rental properties. She was a tiny scrap of a thing, no bigger than thruppence, as Gordie might say. When he reached the spot where she had been drawing on the road, he looked down.

This is my class, 2A, he read. *My best frend is ban.* There was a picture of Ban (Ban? Perhaps he or she was Vietnamese?) with the same alarming curly hair as depicted on her own head. *Do you lik my drawing?*

She had drawn two crooked boxes, one containing the letter Y and the other containing the letter N, and beneath them, two further boxes, empty, with a pointing arrow and a misspelled word, *Ansa*. Jonathan looked around for any remaining chalk but there was none. He kicked his sandal among the stones and little rocks, looking for a soft one, so that he might write his answer. The first he picked up was no good, nor the second, but finally he came upon a small rock of gluey, orangey clay.

Kneeling, he scratched a big fat tick under the box for Y. For good measure, he wrote out the word YES in large letters underneath, followed by three exclamation marks. He hoped it would be visible in the morning.

Sylv, stranded unsmiling behind the counter of the shop, watched him come in. She was not about to show that she was impressed by anyone or anything, and especially not by him. Rich, was he? Good-looking? Hadn't his wife left him for a woman? He must be hopeless in the sack. She felt an agreeable prick of *schadenfreude*: ever since Jonathan had tried to charge her for using his empty house she had known him for exactly what he was. Besides, she knew something he didn't know, and when he found out, he was not going to be happy.

'No dogs allowed in the shop,' she said.

'And hello to you too, Sylv,' he said. 'Can't you make an exception for Bites?'

'No exceptions,' she said, *like the high-season rental charge on your bloody house.*

He led the dog outside, telling her to wait. She may or may not be there when he came outside again.

'Excellent work on the toilet block,' he said. 'Now where are you hiding the onions?'

'Where they always are,' she said.

He decided against making a crack about their price, found them, and took them to the counter. Two large onions might cost the best part of ten bucks and possibly more; Phil and Sylv held the village to ransom, knowing full well they were the sole traders everyone was forced to go to in an emergency. Sylv put them on the weighing machine, a fascinating exercise in the genius of human engineering; her chair placed just so, within reach of the swing of her huge right arm with its drooping sack of flesh, swinging, like a filled bag of sand. He was mesmerised.

The door opened and a woman came in, her hair in filthy Rasta dreadlocks down to her waist, no shoes. She looked unwell, in need of a decent feed; behind her stood the child, Giselle. He smiled at the little girl but she showed no hint of recognition and did not smile back.

'Evenin', Sylv,' the woman said. 'Say hello, Giselle.'

'Hello,' said Giselle.

Jonathan was unsure of the etiquette; would the mother think he was an old perv if he talked to Giselle? He wanted to tell her that he was a big fan of her artwork but he was not sure how this would be taken, so he stayed silent. The woman was standing there, possibly reading the menu above Sylv's head, an uninspiring list of pies, sausage rolls, seafood basket (for two), hamburgers and assorted sandwiches (freshly made).

'Kitchen's closed,' said Sylv.

The woman seemed to be waiting for something; perhaps she was waiting for him to leave. Giselle was inspecting the tempting array of lollies kept at the counter. 'Mum,' she said, 'can I have a Wagon Wheel?'

A Wagon Wheel! Did they still make them? 'My favourite,' said Jonathan, taking his onions and his change. 'I used to buy one every day after school.'

'Redskins were my fave,' said the woman. 'And milk bottles and bananas and them pink and white ones, what were they called again? Strawberries and cream?' She had a deep smoker's voice, rough as guts, and the broadest working-class Australian accent he had heard in some time.

'Come on, Giselle. See youse,' the woman said, turning and walking away. 'Say goodbye, Giselle,' she said at the door.

'Goodbye,' said Giselle.

'Thanks, Sylv,' he said, turning to leave too. He was not going to ask.

'Mum's an ex-druggie,' Sylv said. 'Boyfriend committed suicide. She's staying with Jules.'

Could everyone's life be reduced to a couple of lines? Would he be *Jonathan, whose wife ran off*? What of the teeming kingdom of which he was comprised, frail in its particulars, impossible to name, the hundreds and thousands of hours of compromises and hesitations and moments of bad faith, those bright flares of illumination, of wanting two things at once? What of the great stream of complicated decisions and inconsistencies and seemingly insubstantial moments that had turned his life this way instead of that? He should have taken off and seen the world, just as Sarah wanted; he should have agreed to the packing up of their lives, tossing caution to the wind, turning their faces to the tremulous unknown.

'Poor kid, eh,' he said. He thought of his own daughters: Madeleine, proud, stiff-backed, and soft-hearted, wayward Amanda.

'Oh, she's all right,' said Sylv. 'Tough as old boots, like all kids. They survive.'

Do they? He saw Giselle's small triangle of a face, her knotted hair. *This is me.*

Outside there was no trace of Bites.

Back at home, he continued with his preparations: he had brought the main ingredients up in an esky. He steamed asparagus with snow peas and haricot vert, intending to pour over everything a little dressing he had invented, using the merest drip of walnut oil. He removed fat, ripe cheeses from the fridge; a nice stinky blue, a runny Tasmanian brie and a hard cheese he had originally tasted on a mountainside in the French Pyrenees, sitting with his legs in the grass after a long day's solitary hiking, the cheese, a stick of bread and a bottle of red he drank straight from the bottle. He had never tasted anything finer—the cheese, the bread, the wine—and it was the first time the air had moved freely in his chest again since Sarah left him. He could have stayed in that grass all the days of his life except that he was a man of responsibilities and his real life was far away. Everyone he loved was in Brisbane so there was nothing for it but to stand up and walk down the mountain.

ELEVEN

New Australian

Marie, watching the six o'clock news, made an annoying tsk-tsking sound with her tongue which Penny heard, magnified, from the kitchen. 'Those Muzzies are trouble,' she said. She rubbed the sore lump which was burning; inflamed.

Penny poured herself a gin and tonic, double-strength. 'That's a bit rich coming from you. And don't call them Muzzies, Marie. You make them sound like mosquitoes.'

'Mozzies, Muzzies. Same thing.'

Penny walked into the lounge room. 'Seriously? A mosquito is the same thing as a Muslim?'

'Don't be smart, Penny. A mosquito is a nuisance, buzzing around, nothing to do except annoy people.'

Penny sighed. 'Just like a Muslim.'

Marie took her eyes from the television. 'These Muzzies come here because they don't like life in their country. Then they want to change our country into one just like the one they left.'

Was it worth taking this on? She knew her mother had her own unexamined reasons for being harsh about Muslims, but Marie also disliked asylum seekers (woe betide if someone was both), Indians and—just to be even-handed—Jews. She herself was a refugee! But Marie's life was a shrouded sorrow, apparently comfortless. She was Christian in the way that most Australians were Christian, that is, nominally, a tick in a box on certain hospital forms. She attended church sporadically, an Anglican church way out in Chermside where—for some reason—Penny's father's funeral was held. Penny had long ceased to enquire about her mother's vanished life; she had once overheard Mrs O'Brien asking Marie whether she had grown up in a bilingual family. 'What a stupid question, Wendy,' she replied. 'How can it possibly matter?'

Penny looked over at her mother. 'You were a New Australian once, Marie. I bet everyone thought you were trouble too.'

Her mother did not bother to take her eyes from the television. 'Don't speak of what you don't know, Penny,' she said. 'It is vulgar.'

'What's wrong with your eye?'

'*Ce n'est rien,*' said Marie. Nothing.

Marie only ever spoke French to shut her up.

In Brisbane in 1955, many people had never met a foreigner. Sometimes, asking for something in a shop, she drew a small crowd; children stared at her as if she were a mythical creature, a talking snake. Whatever it was about Australians that could not be known to her and reflected—manners, customs, body language, some native knowledge locked from her—distinguished her as a foreigner. What was in her body shut her out, the accent on her tongue, everything it knew, whatever unknowable thing it was she exhibited that signified the boundary between her and them; not just the entire historical pasts of Australia and France, but the entire past of herself. Once, in the house where Marie lived when she first arrived before she moved in with the McCanns, a boarding house for young ladies in the ridiculously named suburb of Wooloowin, she came down late for breakfast one morning (a dried-up slice of pawpaw from the tree in the garden, bitter to the tongue; a bowl of hard, crusted-over porridge, a cup of stewed tea; everything protected from the flies by little knitted doilies with beads sewn around their edges) to find two other young ladies—Maureen, known as Maw, a country girl from a property out near Thargomindah (how did Australians come up with these names?) and Betty, from Goondiwindi (!)—were already seated at the long communal table. Both were on teacher's scholarships to Brisbane Kindergarten Training College, but they were also saving up to go to London, where their real lives would begin.

'Morning, Marie,' they said together as she sat down, making it sound sarcastic. They didn't like her; they couldn't make her out.

Marie usually ate breakfast first thing, before anyone was up, to avoid Maw and Betty, often beating Mrs Baxter, who hadn't even laid the table, but on this particular morning she had uncharacteristically slept in. When she awoke she did not feel refreshed but overcome by a morbid lassitude, an inability to command her limbs to rise and begin. She lay for a long time, staring at the ceiling, paralysed. Only through an extreme effort of will did she eventually conjure a worm of energy which allowed her to move from the bed.

'Anyway,' Maw was saying, 'I gave him a good clip around the earhole.'

Maw was doing her teacher training practice at a rough school in some distant sun-struck suburb. Marie did not know what a good clip around the earhole was, but she could guess. Her stockings itched, as if they were made of wool. This reminded her of the silk stockings her father brought back from a business trip to England for her tenth birthday, her first pair, which her mother immediately outlawed, declaring them wildly inappropriate. 'She doesn't even own a suspender belt!' she cried. 'How is she supposed to wear them?' Marie begged to borrow a belt from her mother so she might at least try them on, but her mother leaned across the table in a bid to snatch them from her hands, causing Marie to leap up with the stockings and run to the bathroom. Her mother followed, leading to a frenzied wrestling match with her hysterical mother, scratches on her face, the stockings—beautiful, lost, never seen again—flung from the window.

Marie's porridge was cold. She wondered, again, why Mrs Baxter didn't keep it warmed on the stove, ladling it out as required.

'Ask the old so-and-so for a fresh bowl,' said Betty. 'That looks disgusting.'

'That might be how Marie likes it,' said Maw. 'They might eat it like that where she comes from.' She sniggered.

Marie picked up the spoon and began to eat the hard, cold porridge.

TWELVE

Out of the corner of one eye

Giselle had recently learned to distinguish left from right because of a large freckle on her left knee. Miss Wilson showed her, because she kept getting mixed up. 'See that freckle, Giselle? That's your left freckle. God put it there especially for you, so you could learn the difference between your left and your right.' Ever since Miss Wilson showed her, Giselle knew exactly where left lived, and where right lived. She was waiting for similar guidance from God in telling her the difference between 'b' and 'd', the same little curved pouch, the same stem, an upside-down flower turned this way or that. She always spelled the name of her best friend Dan wrong, no matter how hard she tried not to. She stared and stared and still the letters would not reveal which one was which, just like the Richards twins, refusing to tell her which one was Jackson and which one was Jayden.

Giselle sat at the table, doing her homework. She was trying to keep the numbers from scrunching up together on the *left* side of the page, but they kept moving in that direction, bunching up, as if the *right* side of the page was not the place to be. She tore the page up and started over, but once again the numbers crowded over to the left, as if they had all been invited to a party.

'Jeez,' said her mother. 'I never had homework when I was seven.'

'You didn't have Miss Wilson, did you, Mum? She's very strict.' She wanted to ask her mother how to stop the numbers moving to the left, but she knew her mother was watching TV and would not get off the couch. She looked at her mother carefully; satisfied, she returned to her difficult work.

When Giselle looked again, her mother was asleep. Giselle got up and turned off the television. She was hungry and made her way to the kitchen. Jules had not come home. She opened the fridge; unlike the contents of the fridge at home, this one was filled with mysterious objects, tubs of creamy, unspecified mixtures, fresh herbs Giselle could not name, labels reading *gluten-free* on unidentifiable substances. The fridge did not appear to contain anything she could actually eat, so she turned to the cupboard. This was even worse: packets of nuts, seeds, root stuffs, grasses, everything to feed a possum, but not Giselle. There was no sign of a handy packet of instant pot noodles.

Giselle was starving so she reached for the only thing she recognised: muesli. The label, which Giselle read carefully, said *GM-free* and *fructose-free* and *97% sugar-free*, which did not make muesli sound as much fun as a Wagon Wheel. Giselle did not know what *fructose* was but it sounded yummy.

She went back to the fridge and got out the organic milk, which Jules said was better for you than ordinary milk. Giselle was not exactly sure what organic was, but Jules had once been sick and now she was cured, and she said she would never eat anything ever again that was not organic. Jules's other drink of choice besides organic milk and organic tea was Diet Coke, which Giselle supposed must be organic too, but she could not see the word *organic* on the label.

Giselle was not sure what to make of Jules and she watched her out of the corner of one eye, having never lived with an adult who got up every day and went not to school, like Giselle did, but to work. She was away longer than school, longer than the school bus, not getting home till it was dark, declaring herself 'bone-tired'. Giselle had not heard this expression before and had not known that bones got tired. Jules had grown up in Melbourne like her mum, and she knew mum's sister who died, Aunty Pauline. Giselle sat under the table on the veranda out the back, listening, drawing, while her mum and Jules got drunk. Every now and then she piped up to remind her mother that she was counting how many cigarettes she smoked. 'Twelve, Mum,' she said, and her mother and Jules killed themselves laughing.

'She's the fucking thought police,' said Jules, and they laughed again.

Jules had no children, probably because children were a nuisance.

After Giselle finished the muesli, she walked around the empty house, turning on the lights. She wasn't allowed to go outside in the dark, but she supposed it was all right to go out into the backyard, which ran down the hill, fenceless, the garden opening onto the street that ran around the lake. It wasn't even properly dark yet. Giselle knew that from a certain vantage point beside the fence dividing Jules's house from the house next door she was able to see into the house where the two babies lived. She liked babies—no, she *loved* them—and sometimes the mother let her play with them, on the lawn. Once the mother let her walk the smallest baby, whose name she could not pronounce, and she did not tell the mother that once she had wheeled the pram around the corner, she took the baby out, sat down on the gutter, and held him on her lap. The baby was heavy, squirming, and she almost dropped him. 'No,' she told him firmly, sitting him upright, facing her, his fat fists grabbing her hair. He smiled and she pushed her face into his and he slobbered all over her. 'Yuck,' she said, wiping it off, nearly dropping him again. She put the baby back in the pram.

Now she dragged one of the outside garden chairs close to the fence. Standing on tippy-toes she saw into the house next door: the mother, the father, the two babies, the smallest strapped into his highchair. The mother was laughing and everything looked like it did on television or in the movies; lit up, framed, a little play especially put on for her, Giselle. There was the sound of bats, of the rising wind knocking the trees about, the dry rustle of palm trees; dead husks rattling against trunks.

THIRTEEN

A fly on the wall

Marie insisted on walking to Jonathan's, even though she did not feel particularly well. She was beginning to think she had something nasty in her eye but, if she did, she did not want to know. She had taken some trouble with her hair, which would not twist properly, and she was still not completely satisfied it was sitting as it should. Penny waited impatiently as her mother eased her walking frame through the front door, annoyed because Marie had already kept her waiting while fussing about with her hair; actually, she would have preferred Marie not come at all. She was also worried about her mother's eye, which Marie refused to talk about, which only annoyed Penny even more. Showing great self-control, Penny held her tongue and waited while Marie inched her way down the stairs. Penny's house was on the corner of Blackboy Street and Goodchap Road, opposite Sylv and Phil's. Goodchap Road was named for Mrs Goodchap. Back in the days when bushrangers still roamed, the celebrated Aboriginal bushranger Jimmy Cooney was discovered pillaging Mrs Goodchaps's pantry, which was unfortunate for him since Mrs Goodchap, late of Warwickshire, was a hefty woman with arms like Christmas hams, and Jimmy was a slight young man. She surprised him from behind with a length of clothesline and manhandled him to the floor, trussing him up and boxing his ears for good measure.

Penny didn't know this story, but Sylv could have told her. Mrs Goodchap was buried in the cemetery on the village outskirts, built in 1873. The Landing's dead would have returned unacknowledged to the oblivion of the earth, joining the thirty massacred Gubbi Gubbi people buried only a few years earlier in a mass grave a few miles south by the three farmers who shot them—for no particular reason other than that they believed them to be a sort of blight on the natural environment—but for Sylv. It was she who stumbled across the village graves and what remained of the cemetery while out bushwalking twenty-five years before, when she was still in early middle age and not yet a chain-smoker, still holding out hope of staving off the fat threatening to engulf her. If it engulfed her now, so that she was squeezed into her skin like a plump pork sausage, her hopes of resurrection as a skinny woman had long since faded. Now Sylv no longer bushwalked or indeed walked anywhere at all, having trouble navigating a greater distance further than the shop to the car or the steps leading from her house to the garage. All day she sat in a plastic chair in front of the shop, checking out who was coming into town and who was leaving—and with whom—only heaving herself up to walk painfully from the chair to serve someone at the counter.

Sylv, back from closing up the shop, was watching the proceedings from the viewing platform of her enclosed veranda, sucking hard on a cigarette as she observed the mother negotiate the driveway of the house Sylv still referred to as the Collinses, even though Pete Collins had been booted out by his wife and now lived down the road. Phil had already told her about the mother's arrival. She knew, too, that Penny did not get on with her mother. How could you not get on with your own mother? She, Sylvia, a devoted Catholic, had been the epitome of the dutiful daughter, driving every second day all the way to Gympie to visit hers, who suffered from dementia, to make sure her hair and nails were kept nice. Penny had once thoughtlessly remarked to Sylvia that she would rather be dead than end up in a locked dementia ward. 'But every human life is precious,' Sylv said tartly. 'And, anyway, you don't know how it feels to have dementia. Who are you to decide whose life is worth living and whose isn't? You might find you feel differently when it happens to you.' But Sylv had obviously not been tart enough; Penny, who had less sensitivity than a dog, did not give up. 'That's not life, Sylvia,' she said. 'That's vegetable existence.' How could anyone talk like that about a living, breathing woman who ate her custard and tapped her foot to a sprightly song? It was true her mother no longer recognised her, or knew which day of the week it was, or even how to find her own bedroom. She regularly wandered into the wrong rooms or ate someone else's dinner. Once, shamefully, her mother had smeared her own excrement over every wall in the bathroom but, thankfully, Sylv was the one who found it and, crying, cleaned it off before any of the care workers found out. Her sweet, well-brought-up mother; how ashamed she would be, Mrs Muriel Gallagher, formerly of Hockings Street, Clayfield, a proper lady who had all her dresses made by a dressmaker and who still wore hats to go into the city for lunch! Sylv had not spoken to Penny since. Her mother had been dead nine years and now she cared for her mother-in-law, Phyllis, as if she were her own mother, even if Phyllis sometimes made her blood boil, even if Phyllis sometimes irritated her so much it forced Sylv to retire to her bedroom on the pretence of a headache. Phyllis was family, and family was non-negotiable (although if she and Phil had been able to have children, and they had ended up with a daughter who was a slut like Scarlett, that might have been another matter). No, Phyllis was her husband's mother, which also made her Sylv's mother (she called her Mum), and as long as she was alive, Sylv would watch over her. She was proud of herself.

Next, Sylv noted Rosanna coming out of the Raymonds', next door to the Collinses, which she still thought of as the Raymonds even though the cheating husband had moved out. Because the mother was slow on her walking frame, Rosanna soon caught up with them, and Sylv watched as the three women turned slowly into Goodchap Road, which headed down towards the lake. Then she saw Pete Collins and Cheryl from The Landing's letting agency coming along Blackboy Road from the other direction, from the rented house Pete shared with Cheryl, who he may or may not have been sleeping with.

Look at them, joining up, kissing each other hello, as if life were a cheery, straightforward affair, effortless as a song, as if girls did not run off with men old enough to be their fathers, as if wives and husbands were never discarded like old clothes.

Sylv would like to be a fly on the wall at wherever they were going. Where *were* they going? She watched them walk slowly all the way down Goodchap Street, to where it met Bunya Street. Some of the houses in Bunya Street had dual frontages to both Bunya and Waratah Street, so it was impossible to guess their final destination. Sylv knew they weren't going to the Orpheus, because the pub was in the opposite direction. She might have followed them if she could, if her walking days were not over, if it did not take all her concentration and effort to rise from the chair. How unfair it was that she could not eat and drink whatever she liked, that her own body had betrayed her. She was like that old bloke she had seen once on a TV show about an English hospital. A diabetic, days from death, banned from eating anything sweet. And every morning the nurses and doctors found him in a coma beside an enormous bag of violated chocolates, devoid of their wrappers, ravished, just like his body, assaulted by its owner, by choice. It was Sylv's body; she was its occupier and conqueror and she was hardly conscious of a wish to bury herself alive. She smoked, lustfully, her eyes fixed on some hidden, purposeful business, dimly known.

FOURTEEN

Invisible flowers

If Sarah were setting the dinner table, Jonathan thought, she would make sure there were flowers, even if it was only a barbecue. Sarah loved flowers, great rafts of them, floating on tables and hallstands, on any surface willing to support them: lilies and roses and gerberas and daisies and soft flakes of peonies, settling like snowdrift. But Sarah had never seen this house, never set foot in it, and her invisible flowers would never bloom in its airy rooms. Instead, Jonathan searched the cupboards for candles, not poofy girl candles, but thick, fat yellow citronella candles, excellent for repelling mosquitoes. That they were also beautiful was an afterthought; their value lay in their utilitarianism. Not that Jonathan was immune to beauty; indeed, he was susceptible to it, and considered beauty a dweller of that mysterious, numinous God-shaped space. He stood on the veranda, looking back into the lit, waiting house, as polished and perfumed as an expectant debutante, admiring its high ceilings and wide-open windows, the clean, handsome line of its walls, the now-flickering scented candles scattered low on the coffee table in the living room and on the long table of the veranda behind him. Turning around to face the lake he saw the light had faded but the day was not yet extinguished, day was meeting night above the line of land in the distance, a thin crest of brilliance against the expanse of deepening sky. Just emerging, the trellis of stars in the Southern Hemisphere night, that radiant conflagration of the Southern Cross that tells antipodeans they are home; the smell of a storm settled upon the bristling air; the sad wail of curlews. The night's descent, the wash of gentle waves in the wind, the illuminated house behind him, a drink in his hand and, soon enough, the thrilling murmur of voices.

'Mate!' said Glen Quinn. 'How the bloody hell are you?'

'Hello, sweetie,' said Celia. 'Long time no see.'

Jonathan occasionally came across Glen in business dealings (he was a big fish property developer) and he was exactly the same professionally and privately, in that the language he spoke, inside and out, was the language of cliché. 'Deals' were 'done and dusted' and 'young people' either 'went off the rails' or 'sowed their wild oats' or 'were a credit to their parents and/or their school'. Glen and Celia knew where everyone went to school.

'Lovely to see you, Jonathan,' said Celia. 'I was just saying to Glen I don't think we've seen you since Easter.'

'We've hardly been up,' said Glen. 'We've just come back from a month in Italy. Lake Como.'

'Stop it, darling, you're making Jonathan green with envy. The poor boy's probably been tied to the office,' said Celia.

Jonathan had no desire to visit Lake Como, but it seemed impolite to admit it. Celia would think he was protesting too much if he said so.

'Where can I put these, mate?' Glen held up two bottles of Moët, one in each hand.

'Whack 'em in the fridge,' Jonathan said. 'I've got a good Clare Valley Riesling here. James Halliday reckons it's a cracker. Celia?' He held out the bottle.

'I'm afraid my New Year's resolution was to drink nothing but champers,' Celia said. 'And here we are, September, and I'm still going! Would you mind, sweetie?'

'Of course not. But I've only got Australian sparkling. You'll have to drink yours if you want the real thing.'

'I *only* drink the real thing,' she said. 'Darling, would you do the honours?' She picked up one of the champagne flutes Jonathan had set out on the table, just in case, and lifted it in the air, pointing it in the vague direction of her husband. She appeared to be already a little drunk.

'How's tricks, Jon? Not doing anything I wouldn't do?' Glen sat down heavily in a chair. He did not look well.

'I am the soul of discretion, mate. I wouldn't tell you if I was doing something you wouldn't do.' Why did one cliché lead naturally to another? Any minute now he would pronounce those deathless words, 'It makes you think.'

'Oh, don't talk boring boy business,' said Celia. 'Tell Jonathan who we ran into at Lake Como.'

'Was it George Clooney?' How did Jonathan know this stuff? How did he know that an American movie star had a house on Lake Como? He was aghast that celebrity culture had unwittingly invaded his being, entering his system like an incurable virus or an invidious organism. He never read gossip magazines, except in dentist waiting rooms; he never watched celebrity television, and yet he mysteriously knew that George Clooney had a house on Lake Como.

'I wish,' said Celia. 'George can leave his shoes under my bed anytime.'

'How come you're allowed to say that, but if I said Scarlett Johansson could leave her shoes under my bed I'd be a sexist pig?' her husband demanded.

'Because you're a sexist pig,' said Celia.

'Mate, there's no justice in the world,' Glen said. 'The bloody sheilas have won.'

'Have we? When I last looked you chaps still had your hands firmly on the tiller,' Celia retorted.

Jonathan was saved by the arrival of Gordie and Anna. He saw Celia giving Anna the once-over, running the ruler over her as his friend Will would put it, trying to place her. He quickly made the introductions, noting that Anna wore a dress that revealed the curve of her breasts. When he handed her a glass of wine, their fingers touched.

Gordie was making an announcement. 'My darling daughter has just suffered a personal misfortune, over which we shall draw a veil,' he said. 'No-one died, that's the main thing. She may have to leave early tonight because of jet lag. She's just flown in from London.'

'Oh, we've just come back!' said Celia. 'How long were you there?'

'I live there,' said Anna.

'I see,' said Celia, her mouth a moue of displeasure. What was it that Celia did exactly? Jonathan thought it was something to do with fashion, or perhaps public relations, something that required her presence at the opening of Brisbane's endlessly multiplying new boutiques and restaurants, bars and shops selling branded luxury items and three-thousand-dollar handbags. Celia knew everyone there was to know in Brisbane, anyone who was anyone: the leading architects and fashion designers, art gallery owners and directors, the peacocking politicians not yet feather dusters, the director-generals of government departments, the celebrated chefs. There wasn't a name you could mention without Celia exclaiming, 'Of course I know her! We went to school together,' or, 'Oh, Liz—or Michael or Jennifer or Thierry—and I go *way* back.' Whatever work she did, Celia gave the impression that it was terribly important, and that she was a person of great consequence. If Jonathan did not precisely know what Celia's job was, he knew that she once made number 101 on Brisbane's 100 Most Stylish list, because Sylv made sure everyone in The Landing understood the ignominy of it.

Jonathan heard a commotion from the front of the house and looked up: Penny and her mother—on a walking frame—were wedged in the open front door. Rosanna, PP and Cheryl, behind them, were laughing. 'Christ, Marie, can't you wait till I get the door open?'

'Stop laughing, Pete,' Penny was saying, not looking at him. 'The only time you ever laugh is at someone else's misfortune. You're a dickhead.'

'Penny!' said Marie. 'You sound like you were brought up in the gutter!'

'And good evening to you, Jonathan,' said Pete loudly, from the back. 'Your enchanting guests have arrived, led by my charming ex-wife.' Cheryl was still laughing hysterically. Jonathan winked at her and she blushed; too late, he appreciated his mistake.

'Oh, shut up,' said Penny. 'Hi, Jonathan. This is my mother, Marie.'

Marie and her frame were finally through the door; she straightened herself. 'How do you do,' she said, holding out her hand to be shaken. She patted her hair.

'Marie,' Jonathan said, leaning over and kissing her cheek as he took her hand. 'Lovely to meet you. If I hadn't known I would have taken you for sisters.'

Marie visibly preened, as if puffing out her feathers. 'Oh, don't be silly,' she said, smiling coquettishly. 'I am far too old.'

Penny rolled her eyes, being long used to the particular joy her mother got from receiving compliments about her looks. She *did* look different from other old women, in that her face had not dissolved into old age's sexless anonymity, there was a clarity to it; its feminine architecture of bones had held up, the elegant upswept silver hair bestowing grace, a certain artfulness.

'We're out on the veranda, insect repellent at the ready,' Jonathan said. He stood aside, ushering them forward.

As they moved off, Penny realised that in her impatience to get her mother out the door she had left her handbag behind, containing her wallet and mobile. She remembered putting the bag down by the door and only hoped she had put it inside the door rather than outside but, even if she had left it outside, at least the front door was upstairs and not directly visible from the street. She was not walking all the way home to get it.

Jonathan couldn't remember seeing Penny with full make-up on or, if he had, he had not previously noticed. He realised Scarlett had inherited her beauty from her mother, who had inherited it from hers. She had made an effort with her hair, which was swept up atop her head like her mother's, but with a few careful tendrils trailing down. Her face had a compelling intelligence in it, held together by the same good bones as her mother. She smiled at him, blazing, charged; he was momentarily disconcerted.

Rosanna was the last of the group to move off, dressed in a fetching little black dress. Jonathan noted the defined musculature of her tanned back and arms, but remembered that she was also a bit of a flake. She was a masseuse, Shiatsu or something, and once, during a long walk with Bites along the lake, she told him about Japanese bodywork and acupuncture meridians and the flow of energy that helped the body regain its lost balance. The wind blew the words from her mouth and into the air so that she was forced to shout, and he recalled that she also told him the water of the lake was holy. 'You have to listen to the water. It tells you what you need to hear,' she said. But what he remembered most was that she was wearing no underwear; the wind set her tiny skirt dancing, twirling around her thighs and her skinny, panty-less bottom.

FIFTEEN

Pop the question

Celia was grilling Anna, ignoring with aplomb Gordie's request not to pry. She had already extracted from Anna the fact that she was in flight from a failed marriage, causing Celia to talk at length about how gloriously happy she was in hers. 'I've been *so* lucky,' she said. 'There's nothing like lying in bed at night, holding hands with the same man you made your babies with, long after your babies have grown.'

Anna smiled politely. 'I wouldn't know,' she said. 'Gaspard's only fifteen. And Charles isn't his father.'

Jonathan could practically see Celia's ears prick up: in fact, she *was* like a greyhound, he saw that now, all long and lean and pointy, her nose inquisitive and sharp. She had been telling Anna that she was dressed from head to toe in couture. 'The shoes are Christian Louboutin, my favourite pair. Are you here for a while? Do you know James Street? The Emporium? You *must* go.' Anna did not know where James Street was, or the Emporium, so Celia proceeded to tell her. Jonathan guessed that Anna had not flown all the way from London to shop in James Street, but he could be mistaken. He realised he disliked Celia and her condescending air of self-importance; it was a visceral reaction, a bodily recoil. Had she always had this effect on him? Why hadn't he noticed before? Why was she wearing that ridiculous daisy thing in her hair, her long skinny neck wound around with what looked like ribbons? He was going to save Anna.

He moved nearer to the barbecue, a monster fuelled by a gas bottle set up at the far end of veranda; close enough to the end of the long table where Anna and Celia sat on opposite sides. 'You should organise a trip on the lake while you're here,' he said, addressing Anna. 'Do you sail?'

'The last time I went sailing I almost lost my head,' Anna said. 'I didn't duck in time.'

He smiled. 'I don't sail either, but I'm told it's exhilarating when everything goes well.'

'Glen's just bought two rather expensive new sailing toys,' said Celia. 'One for him, and one for our boys. They did rowing at Terrace, of course, but they've only just taken up sailing. Did I tell you Damien got a promotion, Jonathan? He's off to Singapore to head up Hewlett-Packard's Asia-Pacific division. We're hoping he's going to pop the question before he goes.'

'What question?' said Jonathan.

'*The* question—the only one that matters,' said Celia.

'Oh, that question,' he said. 'Who's he going to pop it to?'

'Jonathan! You've met Katie! She's been going out with him since God was a boy,' she said. 'Katie went to Stuartholme,' she added in an aside to Anna, as if this fact might prove significant.

'Stuartholme' and 'Terrace' and 'Churchie' still signalled something to some Brisbane people—aspiration, religious faith, possibly class, a certain self-regarding hope that one's own child might be distinguished over another—a hangover from the city's early days, when political and public service appointments and individual jobs were secured according to whether one was Catholic or Protestant. Anna made no comment.

Possibly Celia was waiting for her to say that she, Celia, did not look anywhere near old enough to have a son of marriageable age, but actually she did. Jonathan thought all women were self-deluding when it came to how they looked, either thinking they were fat when they were not, or skinny when they were fat, or else flattering themselves that they looked at least ten years younger than they were. Too many women pranced around in clothes that were two sizes too small for them, or too young. He admired Anna's discernment in knowing on which side of age she hovered. He looked at her again; possibly she was one of those women who held her age well but would collapse all at once.

'Everyone eats meat, yes?' he called down the table.

Through the volley of voices declaring their carnivore love, he heard Rosanna's small protest. 'Sorry? Was that a no?' She nodded.

'I hope the meat's halal,' said Glen. 'You know we'll all be eating halal soon. You sheilas will be covered from head to toe in black curtains, with little slits for your eyes.'

Marie gave Penny an I-told-you-so-look, a look that flooded Penny with a high, operatic, out-of-proportion emotion. In the company of Marie her emotions were enlarged, perilously close to the surface, including feelings she did not previously know she possessed. Marie acted upon her as a kind of truth serum, causing her inner self to stand revealed—or at least her more primitive self, which predated manners.

'Oh, for God's sake,' Penny said, 'this anti-Muslim hysteria is ridiculous.'

'You won't be saying that when you get your hands cut off for adultery,' said Marie.

Pete guffawed: a loud, rude belly laugh of the kind that drove Penny nuts. Her ex-husband was a zealot stripped of a cause: as a young man he had joined a cult—Children of God or some such nonsense; some madness involving pretty girls 'love bombing' defenceless young men such as him—and after he had extracted himself from the cult and an early marriage, he was fanatically against religion, manipulative women, political systems; against everything and everyone who attempted any coherent system of belief, especially enthusiastic folk plagued by the notion they must tell others how to live in order to make the world a better place. He got his nickname, Pessimist Pete, at thirty; by forty, he was known as PP, famous among his colleagues at the Department of Education for not voting and regularly getting fined for it, for arguing that changing governments made no difference, in the same way it made no difference joining the union or attempting to change world poverty or the human lust for war, because in the ruined world evil invariably triumphed over goodness. The Holocaust proved this, Stalin's dead millions, men who raped and murdered children.

Somehow Penny had intuited her way to the bleakest man in Australia; some suffering in her led straight to the suffering in him. Pete thought feminism was a cult, more destructive than the

Children of God; he thought dedication to anything—especially to work—was unhealthy, a certifiable psychiatric illness, and that human striving was pointless because in the end life was meaningless and everything turned to dust. Yet throughout their long marriage, Pete charged off on a series of new devotions—surfing, Italian, pottery—blazingly overexcited about each new passion. She remembered his fanatical dedication to photography (which lasted longer than most passions), the building of a darkroom, the long weekends he spent photographing whatever it was he was photographing while she was left alone with Scarlett, a colicky baby, weekend after weekend after weekend. She did not complain; in fact, she made sure her responses to his efforts were effusive, flattering, excessively complimentary, hoping that this particular passion might be *the* passion of his life. But he gave up photography, too, devising a rambling, gloomy explanation about how concentrating too hard on one thing was bad for the psyche. She remembered arguing that the world would not have the Sistine Chapel or space travel or the beauty of Rome if humans were not compelled to concentrate on one thing. She remembered Pete's infatuation with sailing, which was how they came to be at The Landing in the first place, after he negotiated a transfer from Brisbane to the Nambour office; how at the shining crest of each new beginning he thought everything before his grateful eyes was beautiful, including her. But to Pete the travel brochures always turned out to be more lustrous than the real, dismal thing, and actual life, and love, eluded and disappointed him; he was temperamentally set at borderline despair, a pessimist and a cynic because his heart was so pure, so willing, furnished with immense, inarticulate hopes, unfulfilled ambitions and unrealised, inexpressible desires. Pete's tragedy was that he could not value what was his, and could not see the vast dimensions of the kingdom beneath his hand; he didn't want what he had, he wanted something better. Penny knew all this, and yet the day came when she could not bear to listen to him complain for another second about the smallness of their house or the smallness of their life together. It happened not long after Scarlett ran off to Paris with Paul, in those sorry days when the very air in the house smelled bitter; she thought something was off in a cupboard, truly she did, and one morning she took every single thing from the pantry and laid it out, helter-skelter, on the kitchen floor.

'What the fuck are you doing?' Pete said.

'I'm leaving you,' she said.

She hadn't known she was until she said it. She was bestowing benediction, granting his most cherished wish for release into something finer.

SIXTEEN

A moist-eyed look

He had better keep the water jug filled. Everyone was getting pissed, fast, Jonathan noted—everyone except Rosanna, who was on what she called 'a detoxification journey', and Marie, who sat, a handkerchief in her hand, intermittently wiping something near her eye. She did not look relaxed, but as if she were prepared for flight at any moment.

'Oh, shut up, Joni,' PP was saying. 'Studies have shown you can take exactly this much of Joni Mitchell before you want to kill her.' PP raised the forefingers of both hands in the air, as if illustrating the measurements of a fish.

Gordie, opposite Marie, was disagreeing with Celia about everything, except that the world was possibly being overrun by Muslims.

'I'm against fundamentalist Islam—but only fundamentalism, mind you—because of its innate conservatism,' Gordie said, attempting to explain the nuances of his position. 'I'm not against Muslims per se.'

'Oh, I am,' said Celia. 'They think we're infidels. It's the War of the Roses all over again.'

Jonathan admired Gordie's restraint. 'I think you mean the Crusades,' he said.

'Whatever war it was. Muslims are always having wars, aren't they? Screaming and howling on the news, carrying coffins.'

'Correct,' said Marie. 'Wherever they go they cause nothing but trouble.'

'I read somewhere that in fifty years, ninety per cent of the whole world will be Muslim, even Australia,' said Rosanna from the far end of the table.

'It makes you think,' said Celia.

'Really? Ninety per cent?' said Gordie. 'That figure sounds rather improbable.'

'It's got the whiff of a conspiracy theory,' said Jonathan. 'Like the where-were-all-the-Jews-when-the-Twin-Towers-fell-down conspiracy.'

'Mate, that one's true,' said Glen. 'The records show that four thousand Jewish workers who should have been at work on September 11 didn't show up.'

'Oh, that's preposterous!' said Penny. 'And anti-Semitic. You should be ashamed of yourself for repeating it.'

Jonathan looked at her with admiration; she had fire and spit, a quality of integrity he had possibly mistaken for vexatiousness.

'It's all on the record, Penny,' Glen said. 'The only part where there's no written evidence is why the Israelis did it. One theory is that Israel was in cahoots with the American government to justify the War on Terror.'

Jonathan saw that Glen was drunk, in that he appeared to have melted, in that he had spread out from the outline of himself, his shirt free of the restraint of his pants, his eyes smeared, his gestures smudged. Jonathan glanced at Celia who, clearly, was not going to be of any help. Her tiara of daisies was askew.

'Who's for cheese?' he said. 'I hereby ban all discussion of politics because I am king of the house.'

'Can I say one more thing?' Anna, whose red lipstick had run, did not appear as drunk as the others. Her voice was low, melodic; everyone leaned closer. 'My best friend Niala is Muslim. Her parents are from Pakistan but she was born in London. During the London bombings she was spat on in a bus.'

Penny's face had a queer expression; in the flickering candlelight, she looked sunburned, aflame.

'That's awful!' said Cheryl. Jonathan risked a glance; he was not proud of himself. How many kisses in the world were misguided? How many misspent?

'I held her hand while she cried,' said Anna. For a moment there was a respectful silence.

'The fact that some of your best friends are Muslims doesn't mean anything, sweetheart,' said Pete. 'I'm sure Goebbels was a nice man when he was at home. Gadaffi was an absolute whiz in the kitchen. Bin Laden wasn't much chop, though.'

'Enough!' said Jonathan. Anna rewarded him with a moist-eyed look.

'Can we talk about how many wives we'll be allowed to have under sharia law?' said Pete, blundering on. 'I'm requesting four.'

'One's enough, mate. One's too fucking much,' said Glen. Pete laughed; a dismal sound.

Penny was struck by how undone Pete looked, how sadly he laughed. He appeared miserable, one of those failed, overweight, middle-aged men he had once so feared becoming. How had she not noticed before? Was it because he was sitting next to Marie, his former mother-in-law, with whom he had shared so many familial tables? For the first time in years they were seated side by side again, allowing Penny to see how young her mother looked and how sadly diminished her former husband appeared beside her. She had just seen—for the first time—that one of Pete's side teeth was missing: he saw the shock on her face, and quickly moved to cover his mouth with his hand. A broken tooth! He was falling apart!

'I'm getting it fixed next week,' he said, as if she had asked. He looked heartbreakingly vulnerable, unveiled as a child, and she realised with horror—with a terrible drunken sense of illumination and certainty—how baffled and alone he was.

She was flooded with remorse, with a dreadful awareness of her own culpability. How stranded he looked, how hapless! She felt his terror, and her own, and a dreadful new certainty that it was not him who was chronically disappointed by life but *her*. She felt winded, exposed, as if everyone in the whole world had known this long ago—everybody, that was, except her. She looked quickly around the table, but everyone was talking, laughing, drinking. No-one knew, not really, if anyone was happy or sad, if anyone woke with dread in the night. How alone Pete was! How alone they all were in their adult lives, the only ones responsible for their own yearning. No-one knew the most intimate things about her: if she was still taking those anti-depressants the doctor had prescribed two years ago, if she was slowly drinking herself to death. All those years trying to get Pete to go and see a doctor about his depression, when all the while it was her! Not even the red flag of the doctor prescribing antidepressants in the guise of menopause relief for hot flushes had alerted her to her own misery. Was misery too strong a word? She did not know; all she saw—suddenly, terribly, and all at once—were the lies people told themselves, including her. How intricate the lies, how obscuring; the marvellous scaffolding erected around the small, sad facts.

She was too drunk to stand up, but her spirit did; that muffled ghost rose from the table. The smothered thing inside her stood, even if all the while Penny's body remained tethered to the chair. Her new knowledge lay curdled inside her, the ingloriousness of it. Why did she keep reading books as if she was going to find the one book that would tell her everything she needed to know? Why did she relinquish her desire to make a piece of art of meaning and beauty? She wanted to know why the world was so sad; what her mother's suffering was *for*. Who are these people? she wondered, looking around the table. Am I supposed to care about this one, or that? Her eyes moved from face to face; she felt as if she was on the point of some truth, a miraculous clarity, if only she could concentrate hard enough.

What was her small life worth, or silly, self-important Celia's, counting her shoes? What was it all *for*?

Her eyes travelled to Marie's face and straight away she saw something was not right. Marie's head sat at an unnatural angle; a puffiness down one side of her face. Instinctively, drunkenly, Penny stretched out her hand and to her great surprise—the shock of it, her mother's flesh which might be her own; the flesh she never touched—her mother took her proffered hand, holding fast, as she slowly went down.

SEVENTEEN

Anyone who was anyone

Incrementally, day by day, hour by hour, Marie reconciled herself to exile. She was on the far side of the earth, estranged from everything she knew, but the achievement of her exile and resurrection were shot through with an underlying sorrow for the loss of something left behind for good. Her new life felt not quite real, as if it were only temporary, a sort of story or a movie that would soon come to an end. Her lost life lived within her, a far-off land, more real than the new visible world in her eyes. Privately she thought most Australians resembled lucky children and she quickly learned where all their soft spots were, all their hurts, all their capacity for provincial affront. Like a proud schoolchild, Brisbane lay its achievements at her feet: Mount Coot-tha Lookout, Moreton Bay, Lennons Hotel. Sometimes at night she wandered through the solid brick buildings of the city, in search of the opposite of the wooden houses she lived in, where there was only the flimsiest distinction between inside and out, between the press of nature outside the thin walls and what passed for civilisation within. In every house, windows were left open and the sounds of outside—the bush, the streets, the cries of children—poured in; every house a house of sticks capable of being blown down by the Big Bad Wolf. When she stood at the lookout of Mount Coot-tha, holding on to her hat, the city below looked like a great army camp, temporarily pitched, surrounded by bush. Her own life felt provisional, flimsy as a house of sticks; she was homeless, homesick for a home that was no more, a perpetual stranger.

He came to the McCanns' front door, his hat in his hand. 'Prince Charming's at the door,' said Mr McCann, winking.

When she went down the hall, all the McCanns started peeking out from the rooms along the way, and before she reached the door she turned around. Terry and Mrs McCann and Mr McCann, their heads poking out from the kitchen; Wendy and Rhonda from the bedroom they all shared; Lance, Pat, Johnny and little Shane from the lounge room. It looked like a joke, a still from a warm-hearted Hollywood movie, and she laughed. 'Shoo, you lot,' she said, still laughing. It was an expression Mrs McCann used all the time—*Shoo, you lot*—and it was the first time Marie had used it appropriately.

'Marie,' Syd said when she opened the door, 'can you ever forgive me?'

She closed the door behind her. Not speaking, she led the way down the head-swallowing front steps, down the bright cement path leading through the treeless front lawn and out the gate. The heat had not yet faded from the day.

She knew the way down to the river, the river that lay brown and wide and endlessly moving; the same river into which he had landed. She was not thinking straight; of course she should not have gone anywhere near the river, but it was the place her feet took her. Pat and Johnny had shown her their secret camp, where they caught tadpoles and tried to catch eels and fish and where they were attempting to make a canoe. Marie led him there, beneath the cool damp of the hanging trees, where they sat on two upended kero tins.

'I don't know why I did it,' he said.

Still she did not speak.

'Actually, I do know why I did it. I love you, Marie, and I can't bear to think of living without you.'

Doesn't every girl dream of hearing such words? Isn't every girl supposed to long for love, her imagination jumping from love to marriage in a moment?

'Marie?'

She looked at him, his long skinny legs crossed, his hat still in his hands. His face was kind, tender, she saw that, but she did not know him, she did not know where he came from, how he had lived. He might as well have been an African or an Eskimo, so different was he from her. She was shaking.

'Oh, you've caught a chill,' he said, moving closer, cradling her in his arms. It was then that she was reduced, touched, enveloped in living arms coursing with warm blood, her struggle momentarily suspended, her head falling as if in surrender to his chest. Marie Arene, in his arms!

She raised her eyes. 'Yes, I'll marry you,' she said, although he had not asked her again.

'Oh, my darling,' he said, kissing her.

She did not love him; she was outside herself, looking at the girl kissing a strange man in the darkening green, alone, frightened, relinquishing the old, broken part, pushing it away, being grateful and happy to be in a safe place; like Mrs McCann said, *all that was the past*, gone, there were no wars in Australia. She did not need to think any more of the headmistress's office and being told that her mother was dead, or what she was doing that night in London, three days after she last saw her brother, Eric—a *chasseur parachutist*, a hunter of the skies, down from training school in Manchester on a twenty-four-hour pass, getting ready to be parachuted into France, so proud of himself, laughing and practising his bad English, insisting on ordering the tea. She need not think of her father, of the workings of grief, of the sadness that stopped his heart. She need not think of her cousins, those strange and vulgar people, wringing the necks of animals, leaving their soiled underwear on hooks. Was she washing her hair the night Eric perished? She might have been making a piece of toast under the electric grill which sometimes turned on and sometimes did not; she might have been doing any number of banal things. She was so tired. She was tired of endless walking, of endless loss. She longed for that moment when experience passed into memory, for that moment when, without her participation, the years would effortlessly move her from the wounds of the present to a place where the past could no longer reach out and grab her by the throat.

Syd's mother, Min, was not keen on him marrying a reffo. Marie was too dark, too dramatic, too *other*. Besides, if she had caused Sydney to throw himself off a bridge, what other tricks did she have up her sleeve? Now, if he was marrying that pretty little Gwen Harris at least Min would know everything she needed to know: who her people were. Marie might even be a gold-digger; it wasn't unknown for girls to set their sights on wealthy young men, and Syd was certainly wealthy; everyone in Queensland, probably everyone in Australia, knew McAlisters. Why, Syd had served an apprenticeship with the famous London store Selfridges and gained special experience in the silk factories of France! But Evelyn, who taught with Marie and who was responsible for introducing her to Syd in the first place, laughed at any suggestion of Marie being a gold-digger. 'Don't be silly, Mum,' she said. 'Marie wouldn't know McAlisters if she fell over it.' Min found this hard to believe.

They were to be married in the chapel at the Anglican Church Grammar School, known as Churchie, where Syd went to school; a big society wedding, anyone who was anyone would be there. In the absence of a mother, Mrs McAlister and Evelyn took Marie to Gwen Gillam to have a wedding dress made (organza, the bodice stitched with seed pearls; an extravagant veil, trailing six feet). Evelyn and Syd insisted she go into McAlisters after closing hours to choose her going away outfit, which she did, eventually, reluctantly. Marie was amazed that Syd had not breathed a word of how rich he was; an entire shop, running over several floors, hundreds of employees! Standing in the magnificent shop, her courage failed her; she was hoping to talk to him about marrying in a registry office instead but she understood then that it would be a waste of breath. Everyone was making such a fuss; she would never have said yes if she had known.

'All brides are nervous,' said Evelyn, holding up a dress.

She felt sick, faint; she had to sit down.

'I can't do it,' she said.

'Yes you can,' said Evelyn. 'Girls have been getting married forever. Nobody ever died from getting married.'

'I can't,' she said.

Evelyn put the dress back on the hanger.

How could she possibly explain? What could she say to a girl who thought the worst thing that could happen to you was getting your hair caught in the rain without a scarf?

'I don't like being the centre of attention,' she said.

'Oh, everyone secretly likes a bit of attention,' Evelyn said. 'It's just bad taste to admit it.'

'I really don't—I don't,' Marie said, beginning to cry, her courage not only failing her but *running*, sprinting out the door and onto the street, every ounce of will and hope and bravery she had left in her fleeing.

'Sshh, sshh, don't cry now,' said Evelyn, kindness itself, so kind, so very kind.

'I can't do it,' she said again, when she could speak. 'I can't, Evelyn, I can't.'

Evelyn passed her a clean hanky. 'I think we should get the tram home,' she said. 'If you really can't go through with it, you've got to tell Syd.'

Marie swallowed. '*D'accord*,' she said.

She did not want to get married. She did not want to be singled out, every eye upon her. She did not want misery, stockings flung out windows, a son released into the sky, a flower blooming, fading, falling.

They did not talk on the trip home. Their bodies swung gently against each other; terribly, Evelyn took her gloveless hand in her own. Marie hated being touched; she hated having her hand held. Her hand began to sweat but she did not know how to extract it so she kept it there, in misery, the sweat flowing like a fountain from her palm, like a religious miracle. Finally, in agony, at last, they were at their stop. When Marie stood up there was a damp patch on her dress where her hands had been flowing in her lap.

Syd was in his room; fortuitously, Mrs McAlister had nipped up the road to Mrs Anderson's to discuss the flower roster for the church. 'Marie!' he said, his face breaking into a grin when he opened his bedroom door. 'Did you get a dress?'

'I can't do it, Syd,' she said, starting to cry again.

'Can't do what, darling? What can't you do?' He took her in his arms, kissing the top of her head.

'I can't marry you,' she said. She dare not yield; she dare not risk giving up her hard-won self.

He laughed. He actually laughed! 'Which bridge do I have to jump off this time, Marie Arene? The Story Bridge? The Sydney Harbour Bridge? London Bridge? I'm going to run out of bridges.'

She smiled. She was crying, smiling, laughing, and then he took her hand and led her inside, shutting the door. For an hour Marie lay beside him on his bed in the dark room, in a sick, miserable fever, talking and talking, caught in the long unbroken breath of her unburdening, and, as she talked, Syd did not laugh anymore and soon his eyes grew dim from seeing.

EIGHTEEN

The good doctor

'Is she all right?' Jonathan said. 'Quick, Pete, lay her on the floor.'

Gordie, drunk, took a big swig of water before standing up. 'The first law is: don't panic. Stand aside, please, doctor coming through.' He hoped he sounded more convincing than he felt, having drunk far too much for his own good, let alone anybody else's.

When he reached Marie, he took her pulse, which was steady, strong. 'Have you a torch, Jonathan?' he said, already thinking that she might have suffered a stroke. Then he noticed the red welt spreading down the left side of her face; feeling around the bone of her eye socket with gentle fingers, hidden in her eyebrow, he found a swelling. She was sweating; her lymph nodes were enlarged.

Jonathan handed him a torch. He gently prised open each eye: everything seemed perfectly normal. She was certainly a good-looking woman. 'You're all right, Marie; don't try to sit up,' he said as she returned to consciousness. 'Penny, can you please move away?'

The daughter was hovering, looming uselessly over them, looking drunk, trying not to cry and failing. 'Is she going to be okay? Gordie? Is she okay?'

'If you give me a little space, I'll be able to tell you,' he said. 'Buck up, now. There's a good girl.'

Obediently, she sat back on her heels, like a child.

'Penny?' Marie said.

The daughter sprang forward. 'It's okay. It's okay. I'm here.'

They moved her inside to the long red couch in the lounge room. Gordie propped her up with cushions and as soon as she was upright she vomited, copiously, spectacularly, all over herself and the lounge. 'Oh, I'm so sorry, I'm so sorry,' she said. 'I'm so embarrassed! Penny! Please take me home.' She made to get off the couch; collapsing backwards as soon as she attempted to stand. 'Penny!' she said, her voice rising in panic. 'Penny!' But Penny had rushed off to the kitchen, looking for paper towels, tissues, cloths, anything that would erase the embarrassment she knew her mother would be feeling.

'You're not going anywhere for the moment,' Gordie said. 'At a guess I think you've got a nasty spider bite.'

'A spider bite? Should we take her to the hospital?' Penny asked, wiping up the mess. 'What sort of spider? Does she need antivenom?'

'This might be our cue to leave,' said Celia. 'I'm afraid I'm a little too tiddly to drive to hospital. You could always call an ambulance.'

'I haven't drunk anything,' said Rosanna. 'I'm happy to take her.'

'Have you got a dress she could borrow please, Celia? An old nightie will do,' Penny said, swaying, trying not to slur her words, knowing the first thing her mother would want to do would be to change out of her soiled clothes.

An expression of distaste passed across Celia's drunken face; clearly vomit was not on her dinner-party agenda.

'I'll make sure she's had a shower before she puts it on,' Penny said, because she could not help herself. 'And I'll get it dry-cleaned before it comes back.' Vomit, shit, death, decay—all the things no-one cared to talk about, Penny wished to shout about them all. Did Celia think a pair of fucking Christian Louboutin shoes could save her? Possibly Celia was too drunk to notice that Penny's promise was not meant kindly, because she and Glen headed out the door, Celia promising to come straight back.

'Oh, what bad luck,' said Anna, crossing the room with a glass of water for Marie. 'You poor old thing.'

Marie visibly stiffened. 'I'm perfectly well, thank you,' she said. 'Penny, could you help me up?'

Penny looked at Gordie helplessly. 'I should think a little trip to the bathroom to clean up would be feasible, if you can make it,' he said.

Jonathan and Gordie stood respectfully on each side of Marie to help her up. The front of her dress was sopping wet from Penny's hapless cleaning.

'Ups-a-daisy,' said Gordie.

'That's enough of the ups-a-daisies, thank you,' said Marie. 'I am not a witless child.'

'I think your mother is feeling restored,' said Gordie, smiling. He liked the woman's spirit.

The two men led her down the corridor, two courtly gentlemen, each holding an arm. Penny followed, hoping like Christ that Celia would get a move on with that bloody nightie. As they reached the bathroom, she heard Glen come in with it; Anna thanked him and rushed down the corridor to hand her a dress (Penny hoped it wasn't couture).

Inside upon the luxurious bathroom, furnished like a Japanese emperor's, Marie collapsed on the toilet seat. 'I have never been so embarrassed in my life,' she said. Penny saw the effort of standing up and walking had been too much for her; she looked yellow, waxy.

'Stop talking now,' she said. 'Let's get you cleaned up.' And the daughter washed the flesh of the mother, as the mother had once washed hers.

In the lounge room, Gordie was discussing with Jonathan what was to be done. 'I'm inclined to wait until the morning,' said Gordie. 'The poison will flush itself out. She's not going to die.'

'What if it was a funnel-web?' Jonathan said.

'She'd be dead. I'd say it was a red-back,' Gordie replied.

'I thought they killed you,' said Jonathan.

'Rarely. Usually they just make you sick. She'll be right as rain after some paracetamol and possibly a dose of antibiotics.'

'Gosh,' said Anna. 'It's always exciting coming back to Australia. I thought poisonous snakes and spiders were an exotic fantasy encouraged by the tourism board.'

She was in the kitchen with Rosanna, making coffee.

'Anyone want tea? Herbal?' called Rosanna.

'No thanks, we're going to shoot through,' said PP. 'Thanks for the nice night's entertainment, Jonathan. Never a dull moment at your joint.'

'Thanks, Jonathan,' said Cheryl. 'Let me know if I can do anything.'

If he was meant to read anything into this, Jonathan declined. He got up, shook PP's hand and kissed Cheryl politely on the cheek.

Penny and Marie were taking a long time in the bathroom. 'Well, she can't walk home,' Rosanna said. 'Can I borrow your car, Jonathan? I'll drive them.'

'No problem. I'll pick it up tomorrow,' he said.

'Staying put would be a better idea,' Gordie said. 'Her life's not in danger and she'd be better off going straight to bed. Have you got any Panadol? That will ease the pain.'

'Of course,' said Jonathan. 'I'll make up a spare bed.'

'Better make one up for Penny, too,' Gordie said. 'They seem to be joined at the hip.' As a person who had chosen to save his own skin, pulling away from everything that had made him in order not to be the person who stayed, he had a keen eye for dutiful children and for children who kept one eye on the door. Gordie had chosen salvation over enslavement, failing to visit his mother during her last illness, failing even to attend her funeral, having left Scotland by then to live on the other side of the earth. If he had acted wrongly, he was ashamed, but he was still not sorry.

After a long while, Penny emerged from the bathroom without Marie. She shut the door behind her. When she was decently out of Marie's earshot she said in a low voice, 'Look, she's really embarrassed. Can I borrow your car, Jonathan? I'll sneak her out the side door to the garage if you all move back out onto the veranda.'

'Oh, for goodness' sake,' said Gordie. 'I've seen more vomit than you've had hot breakfasts.'

'Yuck, Pa,' said Anna. 'Vomit and breakfast is not the most wonderful conjunction of images.'

Jonathan smiled at her.

'Anyway,' Gordie continued, 'as the only medical man here I'm advising her to stay put. Jonathan is making up a bed as we speak.'

Jonathan jumped up and raced down the hall.

Penny picked up an empty glass and poured herself some water from the jug. 'She'll never stay here,' she said. 'Not in a million years.'

'We'll see about that,' Gordie said, standing up and walking purposefully towards the bathroom, where he paused to knock on the door. Marie must have replied; they couldn't hear what she said, but he opened the door and went in.

A few minutes later the door opened and, instead of turning left and joining them in the lounge room, Gordie took Marie by the arm and led her down the corridor to a bedroom where a bed had been made up with expensive Egyptian cotton sheets of many threads.

'Well, I never,' said Penny. Why could unrelated people say things that people related to them could never say?

'I made up a bed for you too, Penny,' said Jonathan. The implications suddenly struck him. 'Gordie thought it was the best thing to do,' he added.

She didn't have a toothbrush, or any make-up remover, she didn't even have her handbag, which at least contained the faint hope of a tube of lipstick. There was a moment, when she was young, when she looked beautiful any time of the day, make-up or no make-up. Now, she decided she wasn't going to take her make-up off; with a bit of luck, it might hold until morning. She was tired, and growing older and sadder by the minute. 'Thanks,' she said. 'I think I'll crash now.'

He led her to the bedroom. At the door, he motioned her in. She turned; there was a pause, both of them unsure of the etiquette.

They stood for a moment, facing each other, before Jonathan leaned forward to kiss her on the cheek at the same moment she awkwardly leaned forward to kiss him. Their noses knocked.

Lying in bed, Penny realised she was still drunk. The room tipped and, unbidden, her life came crashing down around her head. Her poor mother! Poor Scarlett! Poor Pete! And poor her, lying amid the ruins of her mistakes. She had made her own trap. She felt something in her rise, something she might once have called her soul, a cry from deep within. The noise of life was drowning her, suffocating her; reeling, she sat bolt upright.

•

'That's enough excitement for one night,' Gordie said in the lounge room. 'Coming, darling?'

'You're welcome to stay for a nightcap,' Jonathan said. What the fuck was a nightcap? Even to his ears, this sounded idiotic.

'I'm dead on my feet,' Anna said, 'but thanks for the offer.' She stood up. 'The couch looks fine, by the way.'

He did not care about the couch.

'How long are you staying?'

'As long as it takes,' she said. 'As long as it takes to sort my head out and work out what comes next.'

'She's welcome to stay as long as she likes,' said Gordie, 'although Bites considers her a rival for my affections.'

'Poor Bites,' he said. 'Tossed over.'

Anna laughed; her teeth were white and even; he glimpsed the red, wet gleam inside her mouth. He could hardly ask her out in front of her father.

When Anna kissed him goodbye, she kissed him full on the lips. There was no mistaking her intent.

PART

III

NINETEEN

A girl of air

It appeared that weddings with all the trimmings were the order of the day. Evelyn instructed Marie in the idea that hers was to be a society wedding, covered by the *Courier-Mail*, which would not only record how many individual seed pearls covered the hem of her wedding gown, but how many guests came to the reception at Lennons Hotel, who the bridesmaids were (Evelyn and Wendy McCann, soon to become Wendy O'Brien) and where the newlyweds were going for their honeymoon (a first-class sleeping compartment on the new Sunlander train to a new hotel in Cairns).

The engagement announcement, printed on 16 September 1955, read *Mr Sydney Alan McAlister, son of Mrs Mary McAlister and the late Mr Alan McAlister, of East Brisbane, to Miss Marie Arene, formerly of London, England.*

Marie might have descended to earth on a cloud or been found in the bulrushes in a basket. 'Seems fishy to me,' said

Min McAlister. 'Even if her parents are deceased, why can't we print their names?'

Syd stood firm. 'She has her reasons, Mum. We should respect them,' he said.

The notice set Brisbane society agog. She was a gypsy, someone said; someone else said they knew for sure she was an heiress whose parents, tragically, had been killed in a plane crash. There was talk that she had come from one of the displaced persons camps in Europe set up after the war; probably she had lived for years like a scavenging dog. Balts, reffos, dagos, wogs: there was one Europe, and there was another Europe, and opinion was divided over which Europe Marie Arene was from. She wasn't Jewish, was she? What kind of name was Arene, anyway? It didn't sound very French. The girl was certainly beautiful and she knew what a fish fork was; whoever Marie Arene was, with her fine-boned face and her dark skin and lovely deep brown eyes, Brisbane society had a good look, giving her the up-and-down, a thorough once-over. She had caught one of the most eligible bachelors in town, without any of them knowing, without any of the daughters and mothers among the communities of St Margaret's, Clayfield College, St Aidan's and Brisbane Girls Grammar getting a look in. What a shame for little Gwen Harris, who had tilted her hat at him! What a shame for all the other girls, just as pretty.

Marie hated every moment of her wedding. She hated the old ladies coming at her with their false smiles and their big teeth and hats, the jealous looks of other girls. She hated walking down the long aisle, the feeling that she might faint, everyone looking at her. It was an endurance test, a chance for everyone to finally get an eyeful of the girl who had won the valuable heart of Sydney McAlister. The only thing that got her to the end of the aisle was kind Mr McCann giving her an encouraging pat on the arm as he walked her down it, and seeing Syd's face waiting up ahead. He was smiling, looking hard into her eyes, willing her forward. She saw the intent, the will, the strength of the martyred feelings that had caused him to jump off a bridge. He was twenty-four years old, four years younger than her, but he did not care. He cared only about her, Marie, the stranger, and he cared enough to turn himself into a home.

That dark night on the Sunlander, swaying, rattling, swinging around corners, they lay like children, holding hands. 'You are safe now,' he said. Although she did not believe him, she was moved by his declaration, comforted by the thought that there were still people in the world who believed that safety was a static concept and not provisional; people who did not know that the world around them, even life itself, was counterfeit. The wall was thin, too thin even to be called a wall; everything else was the vanity of human wishes, hoping to remake that which was already done.

Later, they became true man and wife. He was unschooled, she was unschooled; in the sticky Cairns heat they fumbled their way forward. It did not hurt, as she had expected; there was not even much blood. If she did not enjoy the act itself, she enjoyed lying on his skinny chest afterwards, listening to the rapid beating of his heart.

•

She did not know what to do on a beach. She did not know why Syd laughed and said, 'Call that a beach?' It looked like a beach to her; it had sand, and waves. 'That's a mudflat,' he said. 'I'll take you to a proper beach when we get back.' He explained that Cairns was a harbour and what she was looking at was not the ocean. He wanted to sit by the pool instead, reading books. Under the shade of a broad umbrella she was hot and restless, and Syd laughed again, telling her that was what swimming pools were for, to slip into when you got too hot.

Reluctantly she allowed herself to be led by the hand to the water. She could not swim. She remembered Eric pushing her in and, years later, how the girls laughed at her when the school was commandeered by the army during the war and they were evacuated to Keswick, outdoorsy, ruddy-cheeked English and Scottish girls who had grown up on vast estates, walking and climbing in the hills, swimming in cold lakes. Rowing on Derwentwater on the last day of summer term, the stupid little Frenchie had fallen in, flailing and thrashing, everyone laughing.

'Come on, I've got you,' Syd said and she gingerly attempted the steps, where Syd was waiting at the bottom. 'I'll teach you,' he said.

But she would not put her head underwater. She dared not venture further, conceding only to lowering herself into the water up to her shoulders, her frightened little head in its bright flowered swimming cap tipped up to the tropical sky.

They ate in their room most nights, only occasionally venturing out into the hotel dining room. She didn't want anyone to know she was on her honeymoon; anyone venturing a guess as to what they might be getting up to at night. She kept her eyes lowered.

It was strange, awkward, being alone with him all day. She feared him discovering that she was a girl of air, hollowed out. What was she supposed to talk about? He chatted on unselfconsciously, telling her all about the business and his role in it, talking about his friends, or the first time he had seen a black American soldier when he was a boy during the war or about the sacred moments before his father died, and how Alan had squeezed his hand. 'I'll have that forever,' he said. For a young businessman he had a very soft heart, full of feeling. In the mornings when she awoke, he was already looking at her, his eyes full of astonished love.

TWENTY

Vive la France!

Scarlett had been ringing her mother's landline since seven o'clock in the morning and now she was pissed off. Where was she? Even her mobile—never reliable—kept switching to voicemail and Scarlett had left at least four messages. She always knew where her mother was; it was unlike her not to pick up. Hippolyte had been screaming his head off all night; every time Scarlett fell asleep, there he went again. Paul slept right through, but Scarlett was wrenched from sleep so many times that, after a while, the sound of his howl entered her skull as an image, a sort of black, gaping hole, a shadow at the window. The strength of it, the fury! When she thought of the force of the rage Hippolyte carried in his small body, she could not help but wonder where all that fury went in adults. How did everyone learn to keep that rage in? Or did it subside? It certainly did not appear to have subsided in her mother, who, these days, was always furious. Scarlett was forever telling Paul that her mother was a total bitch and she was never going to see her again, and then one of the babies would get sick or have an accident, or she would run out of washing powder, or else she would get so lonely, stuck with the babies all day, she would end up wandering over to her mother's. Her mother was excellent for taking the boys off her hands, for telling her to go off for the day to Brisbane, if it was school holidays and Penny didn't have to go to work. Sometimes she babysat while Scarlett and Paul went into Noosa for dinner (she drove; Paul drank), even though her mother made it clear she did not like Paul and never would. 'I've got two choices,' she said when the scandal broke. 'I can never see you again, or we can remain in contact. But if I choose to see you, it doesn't mean I have to see Paul.'

But of course she did; it was impossible not to. How hard it was to keep hating Paul! He was smart, charming, so dashingly handsome, and he refused to be shamefaced; he refused to be cowed; he was polite and well-mannered with her mother and father at all times. For the most part, her mother ignored him; if she had to speak to him, it was cursory, abrupt. She knew that a dramatic exchange had taken place the night Scarlett had revealed her love; that her mother had raced off to confront Paul, leaving her stranded with her father in the kitchen.

'Life, eh?' said her hopeless dad, shrugging his shoulders. 'It never goes in the direction you expect.' Why did he seem excited, even pleased?

If her father was expecting her life to go in the same trite direction as his and her mother's—disappointment, disillusion, the dull predictable adult entrapments of mortgages and nine-to-five jobs—he was mistaken. She was more like her grandmother, fearless, born for adventure. She was more like her grandfather, jumping into the river of life. Scarlett was already leaning sideways out of the architecture, climbing high and free to a distant rapturous place.

Paul had never told her what her mother said. 'Don't you worry about it, my love,' he said, kissing her. 'You and I are going to run away where no-one can find us.' And they did, they ran all the way to Paris, to a many-roomed apartment on rue Mazarin. She was a quarter French, wasn't she, a fact of which she was inordinately proud, even though she was too lazy to learn the language and had given up, defeated, in Year 10. They sat in bars and cafes and ate the *plat du jour* and drank wine by the carafe (watered down for her) and did not go to art galleries. They stayed inside and made love, or else walked along by the fine mansions on the islands of the Seine pretending to be French, and once they watched a wedding party in one of the restaurants by the quai D'Orléans which was just like a movie. A bloom of white; laughter, waiters in black with long white aprons, trays of glittering glasses held aloft. Light, warmth, colour itself, love was a revelation, and Paul approached love and her, its object, with something like reverence. He was going to count the hairs on her head, he said; she was his life's work. One night they leaned out beyond the curly iron rail which ran around the open-shuttered window. '*Vive la France!*' Paul shouted, and everyone looked up. 'Remember this night, Scarlett,' he said. 'Remember I told you the secret of life.' She leaned closer, so he might whisper the words in her ear. 'It's no good heading for the grave with your eyes shut. Open them. Wide.' He kissed her; it was the most exhilarating moment of her life.

If it was hard to continue to live at such a romantic pitch, Scarlett would never admit it. If there was a first, awful time when she knew what sexual move Paul was going to make next, she never let it show. She was always thinking of ways to arouse him, to amuse him, to turn herself inside out, to be the girl of his dreams. They would go to the Middle East and ride camels in the desert under the stars; they would move to Sri Lanka, where she had heard you could live on less than twenty Australian dollars a day. Lots of Australians were moving to Bali or Thailand or other parts of Asia, countries where you could survive on nothing but air. Paul was in IT, and IT consultants worked everywhere. He was forever sending off CVs or being interviewed for jobs, and if he'd had no luck yet, that did not mean that both of them were not going to get out from under, slipping free of the net of ordinary existence. They had demonstrated the prodigious strength of their characters; they needed only the perfect surrounds to match their formidable wills.

Neither of Paul's two daughters spoke to him or to her now, not even Jacinta, who had once been Scarlett's best friend. If Rosanna could speak to them, why couldn't they? If ever she ran into Jacinta or Ruby at The Landing—they both lived in Brisbane but came up to see their mother—they pretended they hadn't seen her. Once, Jacinta gave her a filthy look and seemed about to speak, but Ruby touched her arm, and they turned away.

She remembered running into Rosanna in Tewantin—she was *such* a massive hippie!—soon after they came back from Paris, literally running into her; Rosanna coming out of the post office, Scarlett going in. Rosanna laughed and said sorry, as if Scarlett was just some *random* she'd bumped into. *You have lost and I have won*, thought Scarlett. They did not speak; not then.

Where was her mother? She knew her grandmother was visiting, that her mother had driven down to Brisbane to pick her up. She had been meaning to go over but hadn't got around to it yet. She loved her grandma, who had indulged her all her life, feeling sorry for her because Scarlett was an only child. Her grandma had paid her university student loan, even though she had only completed only one year of Arts at the University of the Sunshine Coast before running off with Paul. She was the one who suggested the name Hippolyte, which was her father's name. Her grandma was exotic, indulgent, everything her mother wasn't. Grandma bought her a car when she got her learner's; Marie was the only person who kept her head when every other person in The Landing seemed to be running around, gossiping. Grandma had requested an interview with Paul, which he reported went very well. 'She wanted to make sure my intentions were honourable,' he said. 'I couldn't tell her how dishonourable they were now, could I?' He took Scarlett's hand and led her to the bed. He told her once that he was so skilled at cunnilingus because he had watched a YouTube clip of a female porn star demonstrating through explicit manoeuvres upon another female porn star how to do it. 'You are my food of love,' he said, lowering his head.

•

Finally, at ten o'clock, when Scarlett could stand it no longer, she put Ajax and Hippolyte in the double stroller, intending to wheel them around to her mother's house. Paul was down at the lake, taking the old Hobie out for a run; like everyone who grew up by the lake, Scarlett could sail too, but it didn't thrill her as it thrilled Paul and countless others. The setting up was too tedious, the time-consuming tying and knotting of too many sails and ropes; the untying again at the end. But Paul always came back happy; sunburned, windblown, momentarily swept clean of any worries he might have about what they were going to do when they ran out of money. Fortuitously, Paul and Rosanna had bought their house at The Landing when prices were low; there was barely any mortgage left on it, so Rosanna had been able to buy out Paul's share through a low-interest remortgage. They had a pot of cash to live on, paying rent until their marvellous new life in an unknown land could begin.

Hippolyte was still howling. 'Oh, be quiet, *please*,' she said. He arched his small furious back as she tried to strap him in, as only Hippolyte could do. Already Hippolyte and Ajax's personalities were wildly different: Ajax timorous, gentle, easily startled, but clingy, whiny, and devastatingly overactive once he got going; Hippolyte a raging beast, a madman, a party animal. 'Ha ha, you can't get out, you can't get out,' she said in a singsong voice when she had at last wrestled Hippolyte into the stroller, snapping the belt shut with a satisfying sound. In truth, the only time she felt she had any control over them—other than when they were asleep—was when they were strapped in, unable to get out, her prisoners. They could howl until their heads fell off for all she cared; she was the keeper of the key. Mostly, the boys recognised the futility of fighting against their capture, and fell back, vanquished. They usually enjoyed being wheeled about, tiny emperors of all they surveyed, but this morning Hippolyte continued to yell.

As soon as Scarlett got out the door and onto the front lawn, Giselle emerged. Did she do nothing else all day except lie in wait for her to come out?

'Hello, Giselle,' said Scarlett. 'How are you?'

'Good,' she said. 'Can I push?'

'If you like,' she said. 'I'm only going to Mum's.'

Giselle rushed forward, pushing hard, but not hard enough; she was too small, too thin; the combined weight of the babies and the stroller defeated her valiant attempt to push them over the lip of the gutter.

'Here, let me,' Scarlett said, manoeuvring the heavy stroller up over the gutter and onto the road. Now Giselle took control, looking into Jules's house to see if her mother was watching, wielding her load with great importance up the road.

Giselle waited with the pram outside on the driveway while Scarlett fetched the spare key from its hiding place. 'Mum? Grandma?' She went from room to room, but no-one was home. The light in the living room was still on. She was coming out again when she saw her mother's handbag by the front door. Her heart banging in her chest, Scarlett opened the bag; her mother's mobile, wallet, the keys to the house and the car, everything, was inside. Scarlett pushed open the front door, rushing out in a scramble of panic, to find Sylv and her mother-in-law, Phyllis, talking to Giselle. They were on their way back from church in Tewantin and had stopped the car to ask if everything was all right. Sylv was an old busybody, and Scarlett couldn't stand her; she tried never to run out of milk or bread so that she never had to set foot in the shop.

Everyone looked at her as she ran towards the car. 'They've gone!' she said, her voice cracking with alarm.

'What do you mean they've gone?' said Sylv, pleased to have inadvertently stumbled upon a drama.

'Mum's not here! Or Grandma!'

Sylv, who was driving, sat up self-righteously in the driver's seat. 'Well, I saw them heading off that way last night,' she said, nodding her head in the direction of Bunya Street. 'On foot.'

'Who were they with?'

'There was your mother and grandmother, your father and Cheryl,' she said before taking a breath and looking at Scarlett with an expression she hoped conveyed a meaning of deep significance. 'And Rosanna.'

'Where were they going?'

'I've no idea,' Sylv said.

Just then, Scarlett's father drove by from the other direction, coming back from his regular Sunday morning clarinet lesson in Noosa. He was in the first thrilling throes of infatuation. 'What's up?' he said, winding down the window and turning down the clarinet music he was playing full blast.

'Do you know where Mum is?'

'Nope. Isn't she home?'

'Of course she's not home! That's why I'm asking! There's no sign of her, or Grandma, and her bag with everything in it is inside.'

'She's probably driven Marie into Gympie Hospital—a red-back bit her,' Phil said. 'But not on the bum.' He cracked up laughing. 'She might be still at Jonathan's,' he said, when he stopped.

Scarlett saw that one of his side teeth was missing. A spider? She knew her father and grandmother got on each other's nerves. Their personalities were antithetical, in that her father was fatally passive, acted upon, while her grandmother acted upon life, taking as much control as she was able. If Marie knew control had its limits, if she had been taught early a hard lesson in exactly how much life controlled you rather than you controlling it, it was a lesson she had learned well. Never passivity for Marie if she could choose action.

Scarlett looked contemptuously at her father, laughing with relish, exposing the gap in his teeth.

She wheeled the pram down to Jonathan's house, Giselle trotting beside her. Giselle fell away at the frangipani tree, stopping to collect the fallen flowers, crushed, browning; gathering them up into a bursting bouquet of perfume, yellow and white, already dying.

TWENTY-ONE

The responsibilities of mothers

Marie leaped up from the table as soon as Syd finished eating; he had to school her in the art of relaxed conversation after dinner. The doctor advised her to take up smoking for her nerves and together they sat smoking after meals, Marie holding her cigarette as if it were a pencil. 'Darling, like this,' Syd said, showing her yet again. When she took a puff, she took quick, darting sucks in rapid succession, which looked wrong. It looked odd, too, the way she blew the smoke out again, pursing her lips as if she were blowing a bubble.

'It's no good, sweetheart; you'll never make a smoker,' he said, laughing, but because the doctor had instructed her to smoke, Marie felt compelled to persevere.

'I'll get the hang of it,' she said.

Syd smiled. *I'll get the hang of it* was her favourite expression. She had heard it in an American movie and now she used it all the time. Oh, how he loved her.

•

Women were not allowed to work after they married. At first this idea seemed tolerable because Marie had so much to do, setting up the house, furnishing the rooms. 'Don't be frugal,' Sydney instructed, but it was impossible for her to give up the way she had lived for so long. She could not get used to having so much money.

The day arrived when the house was done; the rooms painted, the carpet laid, and the new plastic-smelling linoleum in the kitchen washed and sparkling. The bedspreads in the bedrooms matched the curtains; there were paintings on the wall and a big photograph of their wedding in the entrance hall. Syd held her hand as they walked from room to room, admiring every one. 'The dining room looks beautiful, darling,' he said. 'I can't wait till we have our first dinner party.'

Her heart jumped; she knew she had a formal dining room, but she hadn't known she would be expected to hold a dinner party in it. She remembered her mother, hysterical with nerves at the idea of having anyone home to the flat, despite having a convivial husband, willing children and a maid. Marie recalled her mother locking herself in her bedroom, the endless self-pitying lament through the door. *How terrible it is to be born too sensitive! How horrible it is to be so scorned, alone, no sound but the radio, the ticking minutes, at the end of which lies only death!* How terrible to know that her mother's only concern about the approaching war was that her husband might go off on amorous adventures. How much more terrible to be the daughter of such a mother, never able to tell the truth about her mother's death: that she was not sorry her mother was dead, not at all.

The days grew long and empty. Marie both wanted and did not want a baby. The idea struck her as too dangerous, perilous even. The thought of it flew in the face of everything she knew about families and the misery of them. Then Syd insisted she get a housekeeper, which gave her even less to do.

She recoiled from her well-intentioned new sister-in-law's attempts to understand that Marie had suffered. Evelyn was funny and smart, and Marie was ashamed that whenever conversation turned to consideration of Marie's numbered dead she thought, contemptuously, *Let me tell you about war, Evelyn, let me wipe from your face your smug understanding, your expression of tender concern, and tell you that the more we have to put up with, the less nice we become.* She wanted to tell Evelyn that, in distress, a miserable, cracked family becomes only more miserable; in an earthquake more china is broken than when the earth is still. Even now, all these years later, Marie could list her mother's cruelties, large and small, her floundering jealousies, her limited emotional repertoire. There was no benefit to suffering, no purpose, no meaning. Suffering did not ennoble; grief did not bind people together but only cast them out into separate spheres of sorrow.

Every Sunday Syd kindly drove her to All Saints', a place to which she had become wordlessly, inexplicably, attached, where they sat together in the same back pew at the early Holy Communion service. It was where Father Williams had baptised her into the Church of England in those first lonely months in the boarding house, before she moved in with the McCanns. There was no pardon, no mercy, she knew that; suffering was democratic, differing only in its details. Father Williams baptised her into the new world, into the House of Our Lord, into His promised sunrise; quiet, young, intellectual Father Williams, with his soft, sad voice. Father Williams, murmuring, 'God keep you, Marie.' *God calls us out of darkness and into His marvellous light. Do you turn to Christ as Saviour?* God had not kept them and God had not kept Marie, travelling further and further, her whole life construed as flight. The water touched her head, leaking, like tears. If she was alone, estranged from everything she knew, was it a crime to seek comfort? She thought of her mother: *I cannot feel such pain and live! Who will help me? I want to die!* She thought of her father writing to her after her brother's death, only two years after her mother's, *I can't pray, I can't. I can't forgive the war. I can't forgive God.* The church was filled with sheafs of huge, white chrysanthemums, their great blooms fiercely white against their dark leaves, giving out a strange and bitter breath.

The night her daughter was born the nurses tried to get her to look at the baby. Marie turned, weeping, to the wall.

'Come on, dear,' said the nurse. 'You've got a lovely baby girl.'

She could not look. She heard them talking, was aware of the baby being taken away. She slept. Later, a doctor came in, talking and talking, blah, blah, blah, the wonder of life, the responsibilities of mothers; the baby seemed to be having a little trouble breathing, something on her lungs. Was Marie surprised?

Why had she ever thought she could be part of that commonplace throng, untouched, dumb, alive? She was physically spent, as if she had run ten miles, as if she had swum the English Channel. All she wanted was to lie in bed and never get up. Then, half awake, her head filled with lucid, terrible dreams, she heard the unmistakable sound of Syd's footsteps. She lay on her side, turned to the wall, and the footsteps stopped by the bed. Syd leaned over and touched her gently on the cheek, saying nothing, sitting down quietly on an unseen chair.

When she awoke, she could tell he was still there. 'Darling, I want to introduce you to our baby,' he said. 'She looks exactly like you.' But she didn't; her pinched new face was a wretched replica of Marie's mother's.

TWENTY-TWO

Figure, Asleep

Jonathan was once more woken by the birds, singing him back into consciousness. It was so noisy, the ringing world; the birds, the wind, the waves, the scuttling of unseen lizards in the dry leaves beneath his window, dogs barking, three geckos clicking upon the wall, a frog croaking, a natural zoo. How could he ever have thought The Landing was peaceful? There was a roar of sound: the birds, the wind and waves together making a tremendous racket, as if there was a giant waterfall somewhere nearby, monstrous as Niagra. Outside the window the branches and leaves of trees bounced and swirled, tossed and spun. The wind was ferocious and the shutters rattled, loud as a hundred people knocking. He felt a kick of excitement, as if something good was about to happen, but he did not yet know what.

The wind was so loud he could not possibly tell if Marie and Penny were awake and moving about the house. He pictured Anna's face, then Penny's, the tantalising mystery of their characters. He could have sworn he knew every single thing there was to know about Sarah, every crevice of her heart, every quiver, but he was wrong. He ordered himself to stop thinking about his useless, leftover love for his wife and jumped out of bed, crossing to the window: already there were windsurfers and sailboats whizzing across the lake, gleeful streaks of red and white and yellow glimpsed among the trees. Immediately below, mangroves and waterlilies and reeds rustled and swayed. A few hardy waterfowl bounced upon the waves.

He found Penny in the kitchen, pouring herself a glass of iced water from the water-purifying compartment at the front of the fridge. She looked rumpled, sexy; her make-up was smeared. She started when she saw him.

'Please don't speak. I have the most monstrous hangover,' she said.

He smiled. 'Serves you right, as my mother used to say. I hate to crow, but I feel tiptop.'

'He said, crowing.' She groaned.

'Would you like a coffee? Hair of the dog?'

'A short black would be wonderful. I will be the one dying on the back veranda. *Je suis mort*,' she said, taking her glass outside.

He had an expensive coffee machine and made himself a long black and Penny a short as requested. 'Here we are, madam,' he said, handing it to her.

She thanked him and lay back on one of the two cane sun-loungers, balancing the small cup on her stomach. 'When did Australia become a country of coffee snobs?'

'The sixteenth of January, 1998,' he said.

She smiled. 'I thought it was more like the seventeenth. Do you know the fame of flat whites has spread as far as London and New York? I wonder if we can now officially import them to Italy.'

Her eyes were closed so he had a good opportunity for closer inspection. Her face in repose had a classic, ruined beauty, but not so ruined as to be negligible. Possibly she carried a tad too much weight—he saw that her cup rested upon the tiny castle of her stomach and that her upper arms had the telltale swing of muscle losing its tone—but the bones of her face were handsome, and the length of her spread out was elegant, pleasing to the eye. Jonathan did not regard himself as a superficial man, but he was only human; like all men, he responded to beauty in women. Yet if it was only beauty he wanted, he would by now have selected any number of the beauteous young women to be found at the bars he could frequent if he chose. He was after something else, something rarer, something *moral*. He wished to find someone who possessed that unfashionable attribute which might be called character, someone vivid, entire, not only large enough to inhabit the hole made in his life by the defection of Sarah, but someone as unabridged as Sarah herself. He supposed he was guilty of falling in love not only with Sarah, but with the way she saw the world, the way she experienced it more intensely than everyone else. He had relied on her to make the world brighter and richer, and for a long while after she left, the world seemed colourless and dull. Her leaving made him understand that it was up to him to restore colour and vivacity: it was then that he booked his walking trip to France. It was while sitting on a mountain in the Pyrenees that the glorious, lucid world came back.

Penny had fallen asleep. She certainly had character, he thought; possibly a little too much. He crossed the veranda and carefully took the cup from where she had placed it on her stomach. She looked artfully composed, *Figure, Asleep*, arranged as if a painter's model. She was one of those lucky people who, during sleep, appeared temporarily closed down, suspended, rather than one whose mouth hung open, as if the bound self was boundless, rent. He stood above her, looking down. His eyes registered that she was indeed beautiful. Instinctively he leaned down and swept from her forehead a tendril of hair. Gently, he traced the curve of her cheek. She stirred but did not wake.

Walking back into the house, quietly closing the screen door behind him, Jonathan listened for movement from inside, but there was no sound from Marie's room. He walked up the corridor and stood in front of the bedroom, his ear to the door. What if she had died? He knocked quietly. There was no response: he was in two minds whether to open the door or steal away, but the possibility of her lying dead, or mortally ill, caused him to open it.

Marie appeared to be asleep, but he still couldn't be sure she wasn't dead. He entered the room and stole across to the bed to make sure she was breathing; as he crossed the room, too late he realised she might wake and see him. As silently as he could he crept close enough to witness the rise and fall of her breath. He turned and fled.

Two women asleep in his house; surely it was not too much to ask that one materialise into the woman of his dreams? Must he go through life cutting his dreams order to fit the quotidian cloth? It seemed to him he did not want much; he wanted to love and to be loved in return. But perhaps even that was too much, too impossible, like wanting to be happy—whatever that was. Perhaps the whole point was to arrive at the understanding that the cut cloth *was* life? Perhaps existence was meant to be a half-formed thing, never quite coming together, a trackless forest, everyone doomed to wander off in the wrong direction. He was not unhappy; he was financially secure, well-fed, loved by his children and by his friends, generally regarded by everyone who knew him as a good man. And yet, and yet . . . he was a starved romantic, a secret unknown even to his vanished wife. Jonathan Lott, construction law specialist, senior partner, willing, waiting, surrounded by a sea of womanly choice, in love with his runaway wife.

After he had showered and shaved (in the privacy of his own ensuite), he ventured out again. Marie had still not appeared and Penny—also now showered and dressed, he noted—was pacing up and down the lounge room, a worried look on her face. 'Do you think it's strange that she's sleeping for so long?' she asked as soon as she saw him. 'She's usually an early riser.'

'The poison in her system has probably knocked her about. I wouldn't worry.' How would he know what was normal? He had thought that if a venomous red-back spider bit you, you died in the absence of antivenom.

'I wanted to get her checked out at the hospital first thing. What's the time? It must be well after nine.'

'Nine thirty,' he said.

'Do you think I should wake her? Maybe letting her sleep is the wrong thing.'

Why did women always assume that men knew everything, even clever women like Penny? He did not know about red-back spider bites, how to start a stalled car, how to stop longing.

'Oh, I'm sorry,' she said. 'I'm just speaking my anxieties out loud. I know men never do. It used to drive Pete crazy.' She made a wry sort of grimace. 'What a pair we made, me rabbiting on about everything in the world that worried me, and him rabbiting on about the pointlessness of me rabbiting on. It's like a cosmic joke, isn't it?'

He smiled. 'It's amazing how anyone stays married at all, really.'

She looked at him. 'And yet we keep getting married. We keep hoping.'

They stood, staring at each other.

'Oh well,' she said, looking away hurriedly. 'What's the point of being alive if you don't have hope? The triumph of hope over experience and all that.'

He looked away too, moving quickly in the direction of the kitchen. 'Can I get you another coffee?' he called over his shoulder.

Penny thought he resembled a shy, startled boy, with his rumpled hair and his way of not looking her in the eye, and she was struck forcefully by his physical attractions. She had repaired herself as best she could; when she awoke mascara stained the pillow but enough remained smudged around her eyes so that she could smear it around the rims of her eyelids. These days, left undefined, she resembled a skinned cat, but this morning was one of those happy mornings when she looked half decent, despite her hangover.

'Yes, please,' she said. 'Make it a double shot. I'll go and check on her again, if that's okay.' She walked down the hall, fast.

He was on the veranda when she returned.

'How is she?' he asked.

'Still sleeping. I suppose one benefit of her being asleep is that she can't talk. She can't tell me about everything I'm doing wrong.'

He laughed. 'You'd never think she was in her eighties. She's like a seventy-year-old. She's quite something.'

'Yes, isn't she? If she wasn't my mother, I'd probably think she was quite something too.'

They fell silent, Penny struck, once again, by a feeling of disgrace; not by her mother's illness, but by her own unveiling. She was alert to the proximity of Jonathan's body, of its sensual grace. There was a new, charged tension that hadn't been there before; her hangover did not help, making her hyper-aware, vulnerable, as if all her wordly disguises had been peeled away. Last night was upon her still; what a fool she had been, and was. How was she supposed to present herself now, so as not to appear so grievously disappointed? She had a horror of appearing needy, of being the person who was pitied. It seemed vital to make it clear to the world, and to Jonathan in particular, that she had got everything she wanted. She was happy! Really, she was!

Jonathan was starting to wish he could get on with his day; there was something about Penny that was making him uncomfortable. He had awarded himself a long weekend and he had only the rest of today and tomorrow morning before he had to head off again. He wanted to see about the garden;

if there was enough water in the water tank. He wanted to see if he could talk to Anna, alone; whether she stood up to closer inspection. Then he heard someone coming up the path beside the house and quickly identified the *yoohoo* as belonging to Phil from the shop, loudly announcing his arrival all the way along the path and up the stairs onto the veranda, where he stopped and did a double take at the unexpected sight of Penny. 'Well, good morning to *you*,' he said, a lecherous grin on his face.

'Hi, Phil,' she said. 'Jonathan put me and Marie up for the night because she was ill.'

Phil looked disappointed.

'What's up, Phil?' Jonathan said, his morning ruined, any plans fast disappearing.

'I've just come to let you know about a proposal for a walkway around the western side of the lake,' Phil said.

'What? You mean this side?'

'That's right, my friend. It's going to run from the camping ground around the front past the shop and right up to Frogmouth Point.'

'Right past this house?'

''Fraid so,' Phil said. 'A fixed walkway. Built over the water.'

'Knock, knock. How's the patient?' It was Celia, coming up the stairs with a bunch of native flowers. 'I was hoping you'd still be here. How's she doing?' And then a fearful wailing, a screaming child, and Scarlett folding up the stroller at the bottom of the stairs, sending the bellowing child up ahead. Jonathan stood up just in time to glimpse Giselle below, hiding in the bushes.

'Oh, Hippy!' Penny cried. 'What's wrong, darling? Come to Nana!' And yet another child, being led by the hand by the beautiful, dishevelled Scarlett, a new child, also beginning to cry.

'Never rains but it pours, eh, Jonno?' said Phil, singularly pleased.

TWENTY-THREE

Ooh la la

There wasn't one single, shining moment when Marie came out of her corner, swinging. Her move from the shadows into the light was gradual, uneven, one step forward two steps back, as was her resignation (never acceptance) regarding the facts of her life. She did not speak French to anyone because she did not know another French person—and besides, that part of her life was gone. There was an irreparable rift between her and her native place, between her tongue and its home. She did not look back but forward, never speaking French to her babies, because they were Australian and another language would only confuse them. If language was the house of being, Marie was changing addresses.

But slowly it began to dawn on her that being French was an advantage. The *Courier-Mail* breathlessly reported on the latest fashions from Paris, and one morning at the breakfast table she was astonished to read a local woman journalist's highly glamorised account of her trip to the Continent, and to Paris in particular, where she observed that when a French woman came into a room, 'the first thing you notice is that she walks better, her head and feet are better dressed, her clothes finer and better put on than any woman you have ever seen'. Marie laughed. What was this nonsense? She must remember to try it out, being 'French', more splendid than she had previously supposed.

Soon, little by little, being French became a sort of confidence trick she could pull, *ooh-la-la*-ing all over the place, intimidating Australians, who, to her great surprise, immediately bestowed upon her all manner of superiorities: in fashion, food, manners; in something they called 'good taste', an altogether impossible elegance which they found indescribably glamorous, full of romance, an unreachable quality that could never be theirs. Who knew it could be so uneventful, slipping off one identity and assuming another, the dark airless room in Passy swept from view, that old box of malevolent tricks locked, so far away?

If there was never a moment when Marie stood up and declared *This is me, Marie, if you don't like me, then come out and say so!*, there were many small moments, starting with her first nervous dinner party in her new dining room at Ascot, when she failed to properly cook the roast chicken right through. 'Oh, well, it would be too much for my wife to be both the most beautiful woman in Queensland *and* the best cook,' said Syd, and everyone laughed. She was so embarrassed! The blood that ran out when the chicken was carved, the flesh at the centre of the bird oozing like a ruptured internal organ. She blushed and blushed and one of the guests—the buyer for ladies' fashion for McAlisters, the foppish Mr Stuart Middleton, who was rumoured to be a nancy boy—laughed with especial delight. 'I did not believe it was possible for your beautiful wife to look more beautiful, but look at her! She is charming, Sydney. She is the most charming creature I have ever seen in my life!'

It seemed that the new Mrs McAlister was going to be a success.

She never grew to like entering rooms. She always had to make a little mental adjustment, a sort of gathering-up, an internal call to arms. She learned to make this adjustment every single time, to play at being Mrs Marie McAlister entering the room, ahead of herself, until at last her newly composed artificial glamorous French self could walk into any room, any house, any restaurant, any reception. She supposed she had become like one of those stage actors she had read about, who conquered nerves by pretending to be an entirely different person. She conquered herself by putting her old self in a box and shutting the lid, where that girl of loss lived on, but in the dark, as if with her mother in a locked room. The girl outside the box, the woman, wore the new season's frocks before they arrived in Australia, attended church when she could, learned to smoke and how to make brilliant small talk. She was an intelligent girl, she knew—like her father always said—and she learned, excellently, how to be the new Marie, just like she learned well how to do everything else. All her moments, strung end to end: the first dinner party and then the second, the third, the fourth; the first opening night, the first meeting of the lord mayor and his wife. One year, two years, five; one daughter and then a second; the new sophisticated Marie, far from vulgar cousins; smiling and kissing cheeks and shaking hands with confidence, learning to cook like a *cordon bleu* chef, the most beautiful woman in Brisbane. There was a third child, a son. He lived for two days and was buried by Father Williams. He was named for her brother, Eric, gone to join that long, numberless line. But with every passing year she felt a little safer, even though her anxiety about the facts of her past never left her. The day came when she *was* a stylish, accomplished French woman who could talk to anyone, who could even give a small witty speech to one of the many charities she was invited to join. She went to charity lunches, to the races, to the Moreton Club, where she sat among the fellow wives of rich men, their handbags in their laps, white gloves covering their jewelled fingers. By the time the ladies of Queensland removed their gloves for good, she was one of the most famous hostesses in Brisbane, an invitation to one of the annual Christmas parties she and Syd hosted at the Chevron down the coast one of the most desirable in town. She liked being admired, flirting with Australian men, who seemed to think that her being French as well as beautiful gave them an excellent reason to flirt back. She knew life was counterfeit and her new self was counterfeit, too. She sometimes felt breathless with an inner recklessness at what she, or anyone, could do. Why, *everyone* was fake; their public faces put on, every single day: her sister-in-law, Evelyn, Syd, even sweet, unassuming little Wendy O'Brien. Why shouldn't she invent herself?

Penny and her sister, Rosie, were always the best-dressed girls at any party. They wore frilled ankle socks to Sunday school with white patent-leather shoes, a single strap buckled at the sides. They wore the latest, most expensive dresses from McAlisters, their dresses lined and fitted with stiff petticoats. They wore their hair the same, in tight little plaits, but even then Rosie's were forever coming undone, escaping constraint. Even then Rosemary was practising her getaway, digging the tunnel through which she would travel beneath Australia so that she could pop up, victorious, on the other side of the continent. Bye-bye, Penny, bye-bye, Marie, good luck, nice knowing you and all that.

The girls attended St Margaret's, one of the best girls' schools in Brisbane, a short walk from the house. Penny chose French over German, but Marie refused to help with her homework. 'Honestly, who speaks French these days? A few natives with bones in their noses,' she said.

At parties at home she made the girls carry trays of nibbles, offering smoked oysters on Jatz biscuits, and it seemed to Penny that the only time her mother was ever pleased with her was when important people complimented Marie on her polite and pretty children. Their mother had no sentiment, no pity, no time for childish dramas and no time for foolish memories held dear. She threw out Penny's favourite books and gave her favourite toys to charity the moment she judged her to have outgrown them. 'You are too old for that foolishness,' she said when Penny burst into outraged tears at finding her favourite doll vanished. *'Arrêt!'* she shouted at last, when Penny would not stop crying. *'Arrêt! Arrêt!'* Marie only spoke French to shut her up, when she was at the end of her tether, and soon Penny equated French with the language of withered tears.

Penny knew her mother was different from all the other mothers. Nobody else's mother was French, nobody else's mother was as beautiful or as exotic. She was not like all the other mothers from somewhere else, not like Kris Comino's mother, from an island in Greece called Kythera, who was small and squat and dowdy, dressed in black. Kris was the only Greek girl in the whole school, and when Penny went to the Cominos' house one weekend everyone talked Greek, all at once, and it seemed impossible that Kris Comino could be the only Greek at St Margaret's. There were so many of them! But they all went to State High, or suburban high schools in far distant suburbs; none of them was lucky enough to be the daughter of rich Stav Comino who owned a string of Queensland restaurants and cafes and wanted nothing but the best for his only daughter. Penny's mother was nothing like the mothers of the Italian girls from New Farm either, that noisy group who together caught the tram every afternoon to cluster around the school gates, talking, laughing loudly, so different from her own mother, who laughed loudly only at parties.

Penny and Rosie constructed fabulous stories about their mother. She was a descendant of Marie Antoinette, their ancestral home was a turreted chateau in the Loire. Sometimes, when they begged her, her mother would tell them about a wonderful summer in a forest, enormous bowls of hot chocolate, a box at the Paris Opera. It was clear she came from the aristocracy, and that a great tragedy had befallen her.

'Maybe we are countesses,' said Rosie, who was never as avid as Penny to find out everything she could about Marie. Rosie didn't seem interested, because what was happening to her,

Rosemary, was so much more interesting than what happened to anyone else. Penny was jealous of her sister's attractive ease, her insouciance, her lack of regard or interest in other people. Unlike Penny, Rosie did not care what other people thought of her, which gave her an air of giddy freedom.

'Don't you want to know the whole story?'

Rosie shrugged.

'Really? You're not even a bit interested?'

'She's here isn't she?' Rosie said, leaping up to answer the phone. The boys were already calling for Rosemary, whose beautiful, unexamined life was just beginning.

What was clear to Penny was how irritated her mother often was with her father; how his benign, gentle smile caused her to fly into unpredictable rages. What was not clear to her was that Marie was reminded of her father's smile, disappointingly passive in the face of her mother's endless onslaughts, Marie wishing her father would raise a fist and knock her mother clear across the room, silencing the ridiculous, self-pitying words rushing from her mouth. Marie was nothing like her mother, nothing, and yet here she was, in a room with a smiling husband.

One afternoon after school, just before her father died—one of the many mercies of the future, griefless and beckoning, unknown, ahead—Penny unexpectedly found her father at home. Penny knew the famous story about her father jumping off the bridge and—besides the usual difficulty in imagining one's parent young—she could not imagine her bespectacled, conservative father doing anything so rash. His was the steady hand within the family, the calm voice among the raised. He was even-handed, even-tempered; the only clue to his outsized capacity for emotion were the tears which sometimes ran shamelessly down his cheeks during sentimental movies or when he let out small wrenching sobs while listening to *Adagio for Strings*. His was a closed world, as much as her mother's was; their family life a trackless, wordless place.

'Dad,' she said, 'what happened to Mum's family? Why won't she ever speak about it?'

He looked at her, his expression unreadable. 'I can't tell you, sweetheart. It's up to Mum to tell you, not me.'

She felt hot, flushed; furious with him. 'It's not fair!' she cried. 'Everybody else's mother is normal! I hate her! I hope she dies!'

How was she to know it would be one of the last conversations she would ever have with her father? How was she to know that words fly off, rushing through the years, moving too fluidly, too fast, never unsaid? The words were spoken, her father died, her mother—alone with him on a beach at Umina—caught him.

TWENTY-FOUR

The full mechanics of a
swift departure

Suddenly, Marie. Suddenly, Marie, wobbly on her feet, holding on to the screen door. She stood as straight and tall as she could, conscious only of overcoming her embarrassment. She had fixed her hair as best she could and rehearsed both her entrance and the full mechanics of a swift departure. What she had not reckoned on was such a crowd, an audience comprising half the population of The Landing. She had an advantage, though, the noise of the crying children being so loud she managed to assess the crowd before it assessed her.

'Good morning,' she announced to the startled audience. 'Your entertainment has arrived, but I fear it will not be as amusing as last night.' She looked at Jonathan. 'Forgive me. I was under the impression it was only drunken teenage girls who put on such an impressive display.'

He smiled, protesting at once; Penny leaped up and Scarlett rushed towards her, crying, 'Grandma! Are you all right?'

Everyone made a fuss, Celia with her flowers, which she insisted everyone admire; Phil with his collection of red-back stories, with his unwanted spidery advice. She was made to sit down, she was made to accept a cup of weak camomile tea. Then Penny raced off to bring back the car and it was straight to Gympie Hospital, *tout de suite*, Scarlett insisting she come along too, together with her two impossibly behaved children. Marie loved her granddaughter, but her love did not yet extend to her wailing great-grandchildren, who were altogether too grimy, perpetually covered in dirt and snot. In her day, children were clean, freshly scrubbed, and did not wrestle interminably on the floor or fight over every single thing. Penny and Rosie never fought in their entire lives, not once.

At the hospital, Penny watched with a sort of grudging, withheld respect as her mother resumed command. Yes, she wore a hat to sit out in the sun in the garden of that abominable retirement home from whence she came. No, she had not felt a bite; the stupid nurse at that abominable place thought she had an eye infection! The spider was possibly a resident of her hat; the doctor advised that on her return home she should turn out her hat, all her clothes, give everything a good shake.

'You might check the bedsheets, too,' the resident emergency doctor added; he was a personable, smiling young man from Kenya. 'They are devilish little fellows.'

When he momentarily stepped from the room, Marie said in a loud stage whisper to Penny—who insisted on coming into the room with her—that she had never seen such black satiny skin in her life. 'Black as the ace of spades,' she said.

On his return, she gave him a grilling, designed to make sure he had not bought his medical degree over the internet. Satisfied as to his credentials, she clearly remained unconvinced about the extent of his grasp of Australia's native wildlife.

'Do you have red-back spiders in Kenya?' she enquired.

'No, ma'am, we do not,' he replied. 'We have funnel-webs, however—though unlike yours, our funnel-webs are harmless. Our dangerous creatures are usually larger.' He laughed, showing all his teeth, dazzling against his black skin.

Marie hoped he knew what he was talking about. She still felt slightly nauseous, and the lump on her eyebrow throbbed. She was not dying after all; today was not her moment.

In the waiting room, Scarlett was having trouble controlling her children. 'Oh, please sit down,' she said in a hopeless sort of voice, as if she did not expect them to pay the slightest attention. They were in the children's corner, playing with the toys, which meant they were chucking things at each other. An exasperated nurse kept shooting hard glances at Scarlett, which she either did not see or chose to ignore.

'Come on, Scarlett,' said Penny in a cross voice, picking up Hippy, slinging him on one hip. With her free hand she tried to guide her mother and her frame out the door; Scarlett fell behind, trying to round up Ajax, who was evading capture, shrieking, running around hysterically.

'I'm going to buy you a blue heeler, Scarlett,' Penny said. 'A cattle dog could do a better job than you.'

Now it was Scarlett's turn to fling a hard glance at her mother. 'Don't give me the evil eye, young lady,' Penny said.

•

By lunchtime, order was restored; restored as far as it could possibly be. Both boys were asleep, collapsed like puppies on a rug in front of the television. Further up the corridor, Marie was asleep too, floating upon brand-new sheets, carefully checked for devilish fellows. There was a knock at the door. Annoyed, Penny moved as quietly as she could up the corridor.

'Can I play with the babies?' Giselle asked loudly, her anxious little face a triangle of hope.

'Sorry, sweetie, they're asleep,' Penny whispered, making a shushing shape with her fingers and lips. She smiled, shutting the door.

'When will they wake up?'

Penny opened the door a crack. 'I don't know. We're pretty busy today, Giselle. Why don't you try another day, sweetheart?'

The child did not move.

'Off you go, love,' Penny said encouragingly.

With a sad, solemn acknowledgement of her head, Giselle turned away.

Inside, Penny wordlessly indicated to Scarlett they should move away from the sleeping children and into the kitchen. Fortified by coffee and Panadol and water and fizzy vitamin pills, Penny had started to revive. She shook the image of Giselle from her head: some watermark of shame was upon Penny still but, now, in the quiet gloom of the shuttered house, no-one present other than her own family, she allowed herself a moment of respite. What could she possibly do for the poor child? She had enough problems of her own: for some time she had wanted to talk to Scarlett about going back to study; she wanted not to erase her daughter's mistakes, but to adjust them; she knew enough about mistakes to know some were incurable, even fatal. Penny would live forever with the sight of Scarlett emerging through the arrivals tunnel at Brisbane International Airport, her face anxious, puffy, her belly full of baby, her life undone. She and Paul, back at The Landing, not in glorious triumph but because Scarlett was, after all, only a frightened teenage girl, suddenly in need of her mother.

TWENTY-FIVE

Lady of the lake

Jonathan had swept the leaves from the front lawn, checked the water tank levels, taken a quick reconnaissance walk around the boundaries of his castle. Of course there was no way the walkway would get approval; surely the council or the Department of Environment and Resource Management—he'd have to check but he assumed DERM would be the responsible body—surely everyone would see that while the lake itself and the bit of beach at the front of his house might not technically belong to him, his privacy did. He'd check, too, the precise boundaries; Jerry—the firm's senior property lawyer and one of the other partners—could have a look and give him some advice about how to proceed. While Jonathan understood the disquiet engendered by the continued private ownership of some of the most beautiful squares in London, The Landing was not a private square but an Australian lake: generous, beautiful, the property of the people—including him. The people owned it, except for this one tiny bit, this little private slice of paradise, these reeds, these waterlilies, the harmonious Japanese quiet that existed only because it was cultivated and tended by him, Jonathan. He loved his portion of The Landing, the wash of the waves, the tiny beach; the whole pleasing aspect laid out before his eyes. It was his, he had made it; it was his own Sarah-free space, the first place on earth where he had reclaimed sovereignty, and the more he thought about the possibility of its loss, the more exercised he became.

Jonathan's bare feet were in the water, the waves slapping, his eyes on a red-painted rowboat moored further out and on bruised clouds on the very edges of the horizon. He did not hear Bites approach, and when her wet nose swiped the back of his leg he turned around. There, like a miracle, she stood, Anna, all in white, the lady of the lake.

'If only I could paint,' she said. 'The endless sky, the red boat, the lonely figure stranded in the landscape. Pity there's no beckoning green light.'

'Green light?'

'I take it you're not a reader.'

He shrugged. 'Not especially. Are you?'

'Not really. I prefer the cinema, or good television drama. I'm a visual person.'

They started walking along the edge of the lake, Bites trailing. Anna walked in front, with an attractive loose-limbed confidence, her stride slow and meditative, her long plait swinging gently against her back. Her form was shrouded by billowing white garments, weirdly appropriate to the dreamy, otherworldly moment she appeared to be caught in; she seemed only half present, as if her real self were elsewhere. He had not noticed before how beautiful her voice was, low and hypnotic. He did not know the first thing about her. 'What is it that you do, Anna? I mean, your job.'

'Oh, I don't have a job. I leave that to other people.' Her thin, restless hands made a pretty arc across the air.

'To dull people like me,' he said, smiling.

She laughed. 'I suppose so. I never really found the thing I wanted to do.'

He let this pass. 'Where are we going?'

'I wasn't heading anywhere in particular. Looks like there might be a storm.'

'Nah,' he said. 'Those clouds are too far off.' They kept walking, the wind blowing, the trees bending; Anna, in floating white, her clothes a dazzling, drifting cloud in the breeze.

'Do you think anyone ever finds the thing they want to do?' he asked.

She looked at him.

'Rhetorical question,' he said. 'It's just that it seems to me as I've got older that life is one long series of compromises. Don't you think? You're fortunate if you haven't had to compromise. I don't mean you in particular. I mean "one".' He had better stop.

'Oh, I never compromise,' she said. 'I've never chosen compromise, not once. I'm at my best when the house is burning down.' Her face had a strange, wild look.

He laughed, baffled. He supposed this evidence of intransigence might go some way to explaining the four husbands. He loved the smell of burning.

They walked around the lake, or at least as far as it was possible to go, right up past the camping ground, where they reached the national park which did not allow dogs; past the mango trees, the gums, the knotted strangler figs in the old cemetery, through the screaming forest of parrots, alarmed by the approach of a storm. The blue was dimming; dark clouds blew in, great, full-bellied clouds, blocking out the sun. They began to walk back, fast, not talking now, just making it inside Gordie's front door before the gunfire of rain came shooting down, rat-a-tat-tat, on the dry earth, on the roof, down the gutter. Whoosh, down it came, a full pail from the sky, thrown over the lot of them: the houses, the cars, the poor souls running, the squawking birds.

'So much for my weather forecast,' Jonathan said.

'Pa?' she called into the house, which was hot, muffled. 'I've brought Jonathan back.'

There was no response. She walked into the kitchen, which Jonathan noticed had been cleaned, at least nominally.

'You don't happen to have any contacts for professional cleaners, do you?' she asked, as if she had followed the course of his mind.

'Talk to Sylv. Her mother does house cleaning, or at least Phil's mother does. Phyllis. She's not very good, though.'

'Pa!' she called again, before her eye fell upon a note from Gordie informing her that he was nipping around to Penny's to see how Marie was getting on.

'Well, you can't go home in this. Would you like a cup of tea? A glass of something cold?'

Bites looked from one to the other, a sort of cartoon look, her eyes swinging back and forth. They both noticed her expression at the same time, and laughed.

Then Anna raised her head and her face closed in; her smile stopped.

'I'm not very good company. I know it's unfashionable to say your heart is broken, but do you know what? My heart is broken. My husband, Charles, is the love of my life. He's older than me, much older, and he promised that when he died—he always said he must die before me because he couldn't live if I died before him—he promised he would wait for me in his grave.'

She spoke faster now, to no one in particular, her eyes not on him but out the window, at the rain, at the houses across the street obscured by its fall. Speaking in her lovely voice, her body fluid and moving, her hands restless and fiddling with the sheer white cloud of her dress, her eyes looked glazed, odd.

'He promised he would be like Abelard, twenty years dead, his skeleton opening its arms to embrace Heloise. Love is not far-fetched, you know; love is not an abstract thing. It's not even a myth! It what makes men murder their children rather than live without them. Or their wives.'

He wanted to say *that's not love*, but he saw that she was lost in some deep, unreachable place. He wanted to look away, from the dark, from the failure of love. He wanted to pull her towards him. He stepped forward but his movements returned her to the room, to the rain, to the muffled air.

'Oh, listen to me,' she said. 'The thing about a broken heart is that every day takes you a tiny bit further from the pain of it. After a while, after a very long while, you don't feel anything at all.'

He did not trust himself to speak. He wanted to prove her wrong. He wanted to ask about the man who intended to wait for his true love beyond death, how such a mighty love could falter, but his tongue was stilled, his head drowning in unanswerable questions.

'I'm very good at speaking the unspeakable,' she said. 'You might even call it a core skill. I believe that's the correct term. Don't ask me something if you don't want to know. Because I will tell you.'

The rain hammered down. There was no air in the room, outside the world was drowning, and they had arrived at a point when to return to conversation about tea with milk or without, or the possibility of a biscuit, was unfeasible.

'Look, I'm going to make a run for it,' he said. 'I'm heading back to Brisbane in the morning and I've still got things to do. Perhaps we could have dinner sometime and discuss the meaning of life? Your father's got my number.' And he was out the door before he could embarrass himself further, before he ran off at the mouth any more than he already had, before he fell at her feet in a pose of mercy or supplication. She believed in burning down the house and he no longer knew what he believed in. He was running in the thundering rain, his feet bare, his shirt wet.

TWENTY-SIX

Nana nap

Settled in a chair, a cotton throw wrapped around her legs, Marie tried her best not to issue a sharp rebuke to Scarlett and her blasted children. They had already shattered a glass in the kitchen and one of them—she had trouble telling them apart, even though one of them was named after her dear father—had immediately trodden in the shards. Screaming, convulsing, he was restrained by his mother as Penny extracted glass from his tiny, defenceless foot. 'I hope that's it,' she said. 'I can't see anything left.' The annoying child now would not be parted from his mother and sat hiccoughing in her lap, a dirty thumb in his mouth, grimly holding on to Scarlett's bosom with his free hand.

Gordie had a look at the child's foot, too; the second time in as many days he had called for a torch. 'You have inadvertently become our family doctor, Gordon,' said Marie. 'It must be very tedious for you.'

He was admiring Scarlett's pretty breasts, high, pert, not a sign of childbearing upon them; perhaps only the nipple turned slightly dark. Sitting with her dishevelled locks, her blouse undone, she was exquisite.

'I'm used to it,' Gordie said, reluctantly removing his eyes from Scarlett's bosom. 'I've had a lifetime of people lifting up their trouser legs, boring me to tears at dinner parties with their ailments.'

'It's extremely bad manners,' said Marie. 'In my years at McAlisters I suffered from acquaintances fishing out receipts from their handbags.'

'Indeed,' he said.

'Yes, many women seemed to think I was a kind of walking customer service desk,' she said.

The doorbell rang. 'Anybody home?' Paul bellowed through the open door.

'Daddy!' said one of the children—not the one marooned in Scarlett's lap, but the other one—and went roaring down the hall. 'Daddy, daddy, daddy!'

Scarlett looked up, a radiant smile breaking open on her lovely face.

'The man himself,' Gordie said.

Paul walked in, his loud tread resounding down the hall; tall, broad-shouldered, wide of girth, a triumphant child atop his shoulders. Penny trailed behind him, her mouth a little downturned at each end.

'Come on, team. Home time,' he said. 'Hello, beautiful.' He bent down to kiss Scarlett on the top of her head, while ruffling his second son's hair. 'Been in the wars, mate? G'day, Gordie.'

Gordie was shot through with admiration at the sight of the big, lucky fellow surrounded by youth, beauty, by the evidence of his own virility. He looked like a man in the very peak of health, at the very crest of happiness, a man with everything he wanted. It must be true, Gordie thought, that old joke about being as young as the woman you feel. Why, the fellow was a veritable poster boy for bad behaviour! He looked pleased with himself, insufferably so, gathering up his young girlfriend with her high, pretty breasts, his baby sons. How had he told his grown daughters that he was starting again, that he was having another crack at life and love? Gordie did not know the fellow well enough to ask and was drawn from his reverie by the sight of Scarlett, relieved of her child, standing up. For a moment she stood exposed, displaying the natural womanly flow of her youthful form, her naked breasts. Then Paul caught his eye, and winked. The impertinent fellow!

Penny retired to her bedroom. Perhaps it was the sight of Paul or the sight of Scarlett or the constant demands of small, undisciplined children. She looked exhausted, dark rings forming around her eyes.

'You do not look well, Penny,' Marie told her. 'However, I will refrain from asking Gordon to oversee yet another patient.'

'I'm just tired,' Penny said. 'I'm going to have a little nana nap. Do you need anything before I go?'

'Nothing, thank you,' said Marie. 'I am a nana and I am not napping.'

'Sleep well,' said Gordie, who made it a principle never to sleep during the day. He reasoned that shortly he would have no choice but to enter into that other dreadful sleep from which there would be no waking.

When she was out of earshot, Marie said in a loud whisper, 'She is much too fat. If she lost a little weight she would not be so tired.'

Gordie thought it prudent not to respond to this remark and, instead, enquired if Marie would like him to make a fresh pot of tea before he went home. She was an interesting woman, intelligent as well as unusually handsome for a woman of such advanced age; she carried herself in a way that indicated she was used to male attention.

'You are most kind,' she said. And then, when the teapot was brought back and the teacups filled, she told him about her plan to build a granny flat underneath Penny's house.

'Does your daughter know?' he asked.

'Not yet,' she said, as if this was only a minor detail, and possibly the most inconsequential detail of all.

PART
IV

TWENTY-SEVEN

Musical chairs

For many days, for weeks, months following her husband's death, Marie was returned to that alternative world known only to the sick, the bereaved, the suffering. Turn the world over and there is a shadow world, a place of hurt. In this place, all the terrors of the soul live and there are no windows, no doors. Marie found no breadcrumbs, no thread leading the way and——most heartbreaking of all——no Sydney McAlister.

Many people came to the funeral at All Saints'. By then the small wooden church had a new shiny brick front; by then——like Brisbane itself——there was a brick carapace, the beginnings of a new modern self. A new priest officiated; Marie noted from the deep that he was one of these self-congratulatory types, who somehow turned around the unpalatable fact of a relatively young man dying of a heart attack on a sunny day at the beach into one of God's unknowable mercies. Marie was alone, cast out, stranded again in the dark.

Many people pressed her palms, kissed her cheek. Many people ordered flowers for the coffin and lifted up their voices in song. The mystery of life, of death, was upon her once more, the box open. Where are you, Syd? And the cars continued to drive down the road, the sun rose and the sun fell, day after day.

Was it then that Penny's life, and her sister Rosemary's, were fixed for good? Was it then that Rosie slipped the net? Perhaps this was the moment Penny's fate was sealed, some vital oxygen sucked from her forever. Perhaps she never had a chance after that, perhaps the deepest part of her knew she was intended to be the human sacrifice meant to atone for the insufferable pains heaped upon her mother.

She was a good child. She studied hard. She did not smoke joints when everyone else smoked joints; she did not dispense her body to anyone who asked for it, like many of her friends. She was beautiful, she knew, but she was hoarding her beauty, keeping it in a safe place for when she would need it. She would need it when her real life began, when she unravelled the knot, when she learned how to express the many marvellous things inside her. In the Louvre, aged nineteen, she stood transfixed by beauty, tears streaming down her face, imagining that one day she might touch its hem. She was small and inconsequential, but she also carried within her immeasurable possibilities; at nineteen, they stretched endlessly in every direction. The years carried her away from her father's early death, from the loss of him, and she did not know her moment had passed. She was nineteen years old, beautiful; her life resplendent, unfolding.

Unlike the celebrated students enraptured by conceptual art, video installation and multimedia performance, she was enthralled by figurative painting. She loved the human body and wanted to reveal in her work something new, unquestionably her own. She did not feel she had truly seen a body until she had tried to paint its exact contours, its movement in differing lights, the precise way it was an individual human body, unique, differentiated from the rest. She was dogged, determined, but alarmed when a renowned visiting American artist told her art could no longer heal, it could only bleed. 'A good student is not necessarily a brilliant artist, babe,' he said. She was offended and had no idea what he meant.

Marie assumed, always, that Penny would become an art teacher. 'She is studying to be a teacher,' she said, no matter how many times Penny insisted that she intended to be a full-time artist. 'How can you study to be an artist?' Marie said. 'Did Michelangelo get a degree from the Italian College of Art?' Marie understood culture all right; she understood Europe had culture, great paintings, great buildings, great art, and that Australia did not. An Australian artist was an oxymoron; Aboriginal art did not count and the paintings of Nolan and Drysdale and Boyd were pale imitations, faint echoes. For years Penny tried to rid her mother of her prejudices, taking her to shows and galleries, to an exhibition of new paintings by Wendy Sharpe and William Robinson. 'I don't understand what I'm looking at,' she said.

Like a curse, like some logical, inevitable fable, Penny grew up and turned into a teacher. She made one last, honourable effort to become a full-time artist, but nothing she made satisfied her, nothing seemed original or bold or magnificent enough, everything was only half good. She strove for an aesthetic perfection she could never reach, and every day she did not reach it was a misery, the febrile pressure she placed on herself impossible to bear. She could not transfer to the canvas the perfect illuminated world inside her head; she was her own harshest critic and could not accept work she knew was not first rate. In the end, art had to be wonderful or nothing; there was zero in between. That was the faltering year she was twenty-five and trying to get a French passport, trying to be French, and obsessively, neurotically trying to paint perfection and turn herself into an artist. She did not believe it was a bad thing to be a teacher, not at all; she believed there were charismatic, gifted teachers who changed lives, teachers for whom teaching was a vocation. She had seen such teachers in action, teachers capable of changing the direction of a human life, like God altering the direction of a river, but she was not one of them. Penny was a teacher because she was not going to be an artist. Art was not going to repair what living had wrecked and now she could not find a way to live her life as if it were her own.

She was almost thirty when she met Pete. She had survived being thrown over by the most handsome man in college, a lecturer, growing famous for his art. She had survived seeing one of the college's minor talents being taken up by Sydney collectors and Melbourne galleries, then the National Gallery of Australia and then on to international acclaim. She had survived coming back to Brisbane to become a teacher instead of an artist, only to see her sister move first to London and then to Perth. She had witnessed her mother's transformation from society hostess to businesswoman. It was her aunt Evelyn, who sat on the McAlisters board of which Marie was a director, who invited her sister-in-law to take a more active role, not realising that Marie's native intelligence was so formidable and that she was once the mathematics champion and dux of a girls' school in a desolate windswept corner of Sussex.

Perhaps all decisions are founded on what came before. Perhaps if Penny's father had not died young, perhaps if she had become a painter instead of a teacher, perhaps if she had not run out of courage, she might never have sat on the chair that was Pete when the music stopped. In later years, whenever Penny thought about her flawed decision at thirty-three to marry Pete, she had an image of a game, some sweet tune suddenly arrested, everyone sitting blindly down when the music ceased. She wanted a baby, and so she sat down.

It was not that she didn't love him. She loved him all right; she loved his body, the way they fit together, lock and key. She loved the way he came inside her, breaking with joy. She loved Pete because of everything she had survived, the losses she had endured, all the commonplace, everyday disappointments. Doesn't everyone look towards love as a kind of cure, an antidote to the grief of life? She was too smart to believe she was being rescued, but some part of her must have thought she was being saved, most of all from herself. Pete was so loving then, so willing, so full of tender, soft hope. She wanted a baby, he was happy to have one too, which was not the same thing as wanting a child, a significant difference she only came to appreciate later. Back then he seemed to want exactly what she wanted, but of course he did not. They talked and talked—only later did it become apparent that they did not talk of whatever it was that people getting married were supposed to talk of—money was it? Their attitudes to work? To children? They appeared not to have discussed some vital, necessary secret, those critical words that held the key to successful married life. In the end she was left aggrieved, and he was left aggrieved, by everything lost, unsaid. It was the typical story, the typical, everyday catastrophe, their unhappy marriage an alibi for their own separate, private despairs.

Marie was the miracle. Marie was the surprise. Look at her, learning about the divisions of the board, shareholding rights, buying departments. Look at her marching into the accountant's office, the accountancy firm that had managed the firm's books since McAlisters was established by Syd's Scottish grandfather from Dumfries in 1898. 'But you can't do that!' said Mr Roy Phillips, of TC Phillips and Sons, accountant to McAlisters Department Store for four generations. But she did: she sacked TC Phillips and Sons and hired a smart new Melbourne firm, with its Harvard Business School alumni. Gossip spread: they weren't even from Brisbane! Penny, watching from the sidelines, felt older and more tired than her mother. She could not have said when her life began to seem not entirely her own but, increasingly, it did.

TWENTY-EIGHT

The voices of women

Jonathan's mobile started pinging with messages as soon as the car passed into an area with reception. It was like re-entering the earth's atmosphere from outer space. He felt as if he had been somewhere remote, far away, deep in a dark forest. He thought of The Landing, when he was away from it, as being like that magical village Brigadoon, which appears for a single day every hundred years. In his mind it was suspended in time, its residents halted in mid-speech, their bodies frozen. He supposed this was a failure of imagination, like a child away from its mother who is unable to imagine her existing, moving around a room without him in it. During his first years of school he couldn't believe his mother was at home in the kitchen, filling the kettle, walking around. He suddenly missed her—now—all these years dead. He did not miss his father.

•

Unfortunately, unlike Brigadoon, his office—and the work in it—had not disappeared. He had an early-morning meeting with the Cardwell people, which extended to two hours; it looked like he would have to appear in a big case before the Planning and Environment Court. He found court exhausting; three, four hours in the morning—with only half an hour for lunch—then back again in the afternoon, and needing to keep his wits about him at all times. Then there was the matter of the probity audit on the tender process for a multi-million-dollar service contract to deal with; it was way past lunchtime before he got anywhere near following up his earlier email to Jerry seeking his advice on the proposed walkway.

Jerry was a Brisbane Greek, linked to many cousins, a member of that sprawling community with its origins among the colony's first European settlers; indeed, it was a young Greek woman called Artemis from the tiny Ionian island of Zakynthos who was the first governor's wife. Jerry was affable, a big talker, a lover of parties and lunches and dinners, one of the firm's only two remaining original partners, the other being himself. Jerry had five kids, a deliciously plump, beautiful Greek wife, Eleni, and, like Jonathan's best mate, Will, he had been exceptionally kind to him when Sarah announced she was leaving him for Cath. He was forever asking him to dinner during those terrible first few months, introducing him to lovely Greek maidens or middle-aged ones whose husbands had died, leaving them with elaborate brick mansions graced with Doric columns and no-one to cook for.

Now he opened his office door, and his arms. '*Filos! Ti kaneis?*' he said in his warm, booming voice, and Jonathan immediately felt better.

'How are you, Jerry?' he said. 'Eleni? The family?'

'Beautiful, *oreo*,' he said. 'Now, let me tell you the answers to all your problems.'

For the next half-hour, Jerry eased his fears, advising him of the myriad reasons why the walkway could not possibly be built. He had already sent one of the students down to the Titles Office to get the title deeds and other relevant documents and was constructing a case to do with riparian boundaries and the riparian rights of the owner of land adjoining water.

'Basically, we'll be arguing the common law principle that allows a boundary of land to shift if the natural feature forming that boundary shifts by gradual degrees. With rising sea levels and the movements of water over the course of a century, it's almost certain that over time the lake has expanded beyond the original boundaries. It's still your land, mate, even if it's underwater! The state would have to resume your land to bloody build on it. It's a beautiful case, *filos*, beautiful!'

He was in his element, away, man against the state. Jerry was a natural agitator, a red Labor lawyer in a sea of conservative blue, and loved nothing better than representing David in the fight against Goliath, even if in this case David was a private-property owner of considerable wealth.

That night, at home in his large flat overlooking Southbank, the new inner-city cultural precinct by the Brisbane River, Jonathan listened to all the messages he had saved from earlier in the day, intending to deal with them later. He'd responded to all the business calls immediately, now there were only the voices of women, women whose faces he could no longer remember. There was nothing from Sarah. '*Hi, Dad*,' said Amanda in the middle of them. '*Call me when you get a chance. Nothing urgent.*' Unlike Madeleine, his firstborn—independent, headstrong, out of home the first year she left school, refusing to accept any financial help for university fees or anything else and now working as a highly paid accountant for Deloitte in Sydney—Amanda had tried one year of a social work degree, six months of nursing, and was now half-heartedly pursuing an art-therapy course for children. This seemed to consist of him forking out large amounts of cash so she could establish Amanda's Art House in Paddington, while attending part-time one of the many quack alternative therapy schools which had sprung up in Brisbane teaching naturopathy, acupuncture, reiki and various other cures for emotional and psychological health, including finding one's inner goddess.

It was Amanda who had taken Sarah's defection the hardest, as if her mother had run away in the middle of the night with her belongings tied to a stick. Amanda had been a dramatic child, frequently inconsolable for no reason anyone could fathom, given to melodramatic storms of weeping and sudden declarations of her intention to run away from home because nobody loved her. Amanda wasn't even living at home when Sarah left, but renting a room in one of many consecutive shared houses peopled with various aspiring musicians, writers and filmmakers.

She was always in the throes of a disastrous love affair, but the chaos of her own love life failed to make her more sympathetic to the chaos of her mother's.

He was there for that terrible conversation, the your-mother-and-I-have-sadly-decided-to-separate conversation, when both his and Sarah's enduring love for their children was professed, assured; each of them attempting to hang on to the ribbons of their old life, already floating away, never to be seen or felt or lived ever again. How sad he was, how sad the children were, how sad. He never knew what Sarah said in the months that followed, how she had told them about Cath. He knew only that late one night Amanda had knocked on his door, and when he opened it she fell into his arms, speaking in a rush. 'Dad, I'm so scared. I don't want to have a family there's no category to describe.' And she wept, inconsolably, for the first time since she was a small, dramatic girl.

He phoned her number.

'Hello, sweetheart, it's Dad,' he said.

'What's up?'

'Nothing much. Just back from The Landing. You called me, remember.'

'Oh yeah. It wasn't important. Sorry, I'm in the middle of something. Can I call you back?'

'Sure,' he said.

He sat with the phone in his hand. Did he really want to ring Charlotte, the foxy widow? Or Janice, whose face he could hardly remember? He was tired; he was too old for this stuff. He wanted nothing more than to be stuck again in an old familiar marriage, wearing loose trousers, openly licking the foil lids of yoghurt pots when he opened them, not having to worry about keeping his farts in or getting fat or losing his hair. He didn't want to keep going to the gym, as if he might one day catch up

with his fleeter, younger self; he didn't want to be charming,
to keep polishing himself so that he resembled a sort of fussy,
elaborate canapé, offered hopefully. He wanted someone who
knew everything about him. In fact, he wanted Sarah; he wanted
everything to be the same as before, so he didn't have to try, so
he didn't have to think. Was Sarah right in believing he had lost
the habit of asking himself what he most deeply felt or thought?
Was she right that he didn't want to know? Whatever the case,
he knew he didn't want to go through the same tired old motions
of courtship with Charlotte or Penny or Anna or anyone: he
wanted to lie in bed and do nothing but sleep, not even make
love. Now that he thought about it, he just wanted someone to
cuddle. He didn't give a fig about the moan, the ecstatic moment,
the muscles of the arching euphoric back.

He and Will met regularly for lunch at the Brisbane Club.
Will was his oldest friend from university, an engineer, married
to Lucy since before Jonathan married Sarah. Jonathan had been
Will's best man when he had just started going out with Sarah;
she had accompanied him to the wedding and he remembered
being transfixed by her, by her crooked smile, her exuberance,
her shout-out-loud, life-affirming *froth*. He remembered standing
intoxicated beside her on the green lawns running down to the
river at Riverside at New Farm, which had disappeared once
beneath the great Brisbane flood of 1974, and would disappear
again beneath another great flood almost forty years later. The
river rose, as did love, fulfilling its inherent nature, set to sweep
everything away.

They always sat at the same table, tucked in the corner. Will's manner was careful, considered, and seeing his kindly weathered face again reminded Jonathan how much affection he had for him, his oldest friend. Possibly because he and Lucy had lost their first baby son to cot death, Will had an enlarged capacity for empathy, for suffering of any kind. Unlike some, he did not consider Sarah's abandonment of Jonathan for a woman amusing and sat, stony-faced, when the scandal broke and the gossip and the jokes started, when supposed friends claimed to know the inside story. 'Oh yes, and what's the real story?' Will asked, challenging Michael Carr, who was entertaining the bar at the club one night with outlandish tales about juicy ménage à trois. Will set about putting out gossip as if extinguishing small grass fires: Jonathan himself was bisexual, didn't you know? Or the other woman in the ménage à trois was a novelist who was writing a roman à clef about the whole thing. Did anyone know if Jonathan was going to sue?

'You don't have to ask her out, you know,' Will said now, before stuffing his mouth with excellent eggs Benedict.

'Of course I don't have to,' he said. 'I want to.'

'Four husbands sounds like trouble. She's not even divorced yet is she?'

Jonathan shook his head. 'She's just left him.' He knew this was not strictly true.

Will looked at him, his cheeks bulging.

Jonathan put down his fork. 'I know. I know.'

●

Will was the only person who ever asked him directly whether he thought Sarah was gay all along. 'No way,' Jonathan said. He did not know how he knew this, but he did. He remembered their joyous early days, the hours spent in bed as if in a delirium, the way they breathed into each other's mouths. 'I want to eat you,' Sarah said, and she did; his lips, his ears, his cock. He believed Sarah when she said she fell in love with Cath—who happened to be a woman—not because she was a woman but because she was Cath. He'd met Cath once, a small, plain, middle-aged and otherwise unremarkable person he might pass in the street and never take for someone with superheroic powers capable of destroying entire lives. It was an awkward, terrible experience and one he never wanted to repeat: everything he had rehearsed came out wrong, so that he ended up being unable to extricate himself from the subject of transport policy, Cath being a policy writer for the Department of Transport and Main Roads. Afterwards, he wondered if Cath—with her uncanny powers—would be capable of picking up signs of Sarah's distress, or her unhappiness, all the things Sarah said he was too blind to notice. He would never forget the night she left, how she had uncharacteristically raised her voice to say she'd been waving a red flag in his face for months, for years, that he either ignored or failed to see.

'But, darling,' he cried, 'if I'd known, I would have done something!'

'Oh, Johnny, you're so hopeless,' she said, her voice deflating. 'I wish I didn't love you.'

'Then why are you leaving?'

'Because I need to find out who I am without you. Because I need something more.'

She crossed the room and took his hands. 'Because I have to,' she said sadly, unwillingly, as if someone was making her do it.

TWENTY-NINE

A free pass to heaven

'What do you mean she's been bitten by a red-back?'

'She's been bitten by a red-back, that's what I mean,' said Penny.

'How?'

Which part of this conversation did her sister not understand? Was it the middle of the night way over there on the other side of Australia, which might as well have been India it was so fucking far away?

'Earth to Rosie,' she said, because her sister was driving her mad. It was a mystery to Penny how her own life was so crooked, how often she was knocked flat, and how Rosie— from the same crooked family—lived with such unblinking confidence. 'Look, Marie's recovering well,' she said. 'But we're going to have to do something about where she's going to live. She can't stay here.'

'Why not? I mean, really, Penny, why not? Scarlett's made a scarlet woman of herself and you've given PP the flick; the house is empty, apart from the red-backs.' She guffawed.

'Your house is empty too!'

'I've got Russell. He's worth at least two Maries.'

Penny could hardly speak, she was so choked with rage. Was she going to live out the rest of her years with her mother, two old bats taking their regular afternoon constitutional around the lake? Why couldn't Marie go quietly into that good night like the rest? Why couldn't she settle down to daytime television and the *Women's Weekly* and be like every other old woman, worrying about whether the pretty new Duchess of Cambridge was going to make a suitable Queen of England? Of course she wouldn't, not Marie, who had never cared for the *Women's Weekly* or the trials of the English monarchy. Marie required fast internet connection and a computer in her room, so she could do her online banking and monitor her share portfolio. Her mother showed no signs of flagging; she was indefatigable, formidable as an octogenarian media baron! Indeed, she showed every sign of living until she was a hundred and three, like a media baron's mother, full of dash till the last. Apart from her old legs, her health was excellent. Recently she'd had her sugar levels checked, her cholesterol, her heart; the doctor said that everything was in such good nick she could easily pass for a woman fifteen years younger. At this rate, her mother would outlive her; Penny would be the one who died, killed by the rage of exhaustion.

'Are you still there?' Rosemary asked.

'Barely,' she replied.

'It's obvious she can't come to Perth. She doesn't know anyone here.'

'She doesn't know anyone in Brisbane either! Or here. All her friends are dead.' Penny did not think it was worth mentioning Wendy O'Brien, that poor put-upon soul, a widow who had nursed her ailing husband, Ken, for some years before his death. In fact, Penny was due to pick Mrs O'Brien up soon from Pomona station; the old dear was coming up from Brisbane to see Marie, her voice trembling on the telephone, hoping she wouldn't be putting Penny out by asking for a lift from the station.

'Well, we'll just have to find another nursing home,' said Rosie.

'You mean I will. I'll be the one schlepping around for the next six weeks trying to find one that'll take her. I've got to go back to work next week.'

'You'll get a free pass to heaven, sweetie.'

Penny breathed out, hard, through her mouth.

'The Chinese are very dutiful towards their elderly, aren't they?' Rosie went on. 'I suppose it's a facet of ancestor worship. Did you see that thing on the *7.30 Report* about that German guy—or maybe he's Swiss—who's establishing luxury resorts in Thailand for Alzheimer's patients? It costs a fortune for in-house care in Germany apparently, but in Thailand the old folk get their own personal nurse, who lives with them day in day out for a fraction of the cost. They become part of the nurse's family. You know what the Thais are like, so amazingly warm, so friendly.'

'Yeah, I've noticed young destitute Thai girls and boys are friendly towards old European men too. Poor Thailand. Now the west is outsourcing its old people as well as its sexual services.'

'Well, you know, it's a growing problem, the ageing world population. The only people going at it like rabbits and still popping out babies by the dozen are Mexicans. Oh, and Scarlett.'

Penny hung up. Fuck Rosemary.

She was full of fury, she was alive with a raw energy, volatile as electricity. She had to move, she had to walk; she had to get out of the house. She rushed from the room and out the door, banging it on her way out, walking fast down the road. Was it Scarlett? Her mother? Her sister? Which part of her stupid fucking life made her angriest? How dare Rosemary make cracks about Scarlett, as if she, Penny, didn't have her heart broken over it every single day! She had thought she had accommodated herself to it as best she could, given that Scarlett was alive, breathing, not dead from drugs or a car accident or any of the many dreadful things young people died from. She was not a junkie or an alcoholic, she was a healthy young woman who could still make something worthwhile of her life. How was Penny to know if Scarlett hadn't already made something worthwhile, if those two babies weren't equal—or even worth *more*—than all the other supposedly worthwhile wordly things? How do you weigh a baby? How do you measure value, or success? She walked on, hoping that if she walked far enough or long enough or hard enough she might walk out of the anger that even she knew was a substitute for something else; as if she might walk her way out of the painful riddle of being alive.

When she had marched so far that her T-shirt was dark with sweat and the hair on the nape of her neck slick and clinging, she had succeeded only in transforming boiling rage into a simmer. It was even faintly amusing—in a sick sort of way—to consider that in one generation the idea of what was valuable in the life of a woman had altered so profoundly. While no doubt certain sections of society still viewed the lives of childless, unmarried women as sad affairs, many more regarded women stuck at home with children and no fulfilling career—or even an unfulfilling one—as pitiable. Oh, Penny knew there was some sort of stand-off going on between mothers who worked and mothers who didn't, and that American religious fundamentalists and the extreme right had elevated stay-at-home mothers into contemporary saints, but perhaps she had to find a new way of thinking about Scarlett. Perhaps she had to see her daughter as a stranger might. Hello, there's a beautiful girl. And just look at her beautiful children. Such perfection, she knew; oh, Penny saw, such perfection.

She realised Giselle was following her. Did no-one care about that damn child? She picked up her pace, growing cross again. But as she marched on, her conscience got the better of her. Should she call the Department of Social Services? That might possibly be worse. She slowed down, allowing the girl to catch up.

'And where are you off to today, young madam?'

She was barefoot, her feet brown and hard.

'I'm building a cubby,' Giselle said. 'Do you want to see it?'

'Not today, sweetheart. I've got a million things to do.'

The child ran off, the long stick she was carrying trailing behind her in the dirt.

When she got back to the house, Marie was still in her chair, her eyes closed. Penny was pierced by pity, a great knot of it, in the centre of her chest. Her mother was so completely and utterly herself! Her secrets, her vanity, her energy, her formidable will; she was forcefully present, intransigent as weather. She *would* probably live till she was one hundred and three, really, she might; no-one knew if longevity was in Marie's genes on her mother's side, because her mother had died so young.

She sensed Penny's presence and opened her eyes. 'A cup of tea?' Penny asked.

'I'm awash with tea,' Marie replied. 'What time is Wendy's train?'

'Oh, bugger,' Penny said, looking around for the car keys. She wouldn't have time to get changed.

The poor old thing was waiting at the station, sitting bent over on a bench, her handbag clasped in her lap.

'Hello, Mrs O'Brien,' Penny said. 'Sorry to keep you waiting.' Penny didn't address many men or women as 'Mr' or 'Mrs' but found it ridiculous to call the tiny old woman 'Wendy'. It was the name of a girl; more specifically, the name of the girl in *Peter Pan* and—from memory—a name invented by the author himself which became wildly popular on the heels of his book. This Wendy was immaculately dressed, a girl grown old, a girl from another century. Penny had known Mrs O'Brien all her life; her late husband, Ken, a practical joker, was always making her look behind or look up or flicking tea-towels at her legs when he came to stay at one of the units they owned down the coast when she was growing up. He was full of gnomic expressions—*the bigger the hat, the smaller the farm* and *better to be down on your luck than up yourself*—and he and Mrs O'Brien couldn't have kiddies. They'd adopted Shane and Troy, but Shane was a bad 'un, something in the blood, something that led him from a spot of harmless shoplifting and minor burglary directly to armed robbery and jail. Penny hadn't heard anything of Shane for years but she knew all about Troy and Denise and their three lovely children.

Mrs O'Brien walked with a stick and took a long while to move off the platform and down the ramp and across to the car. Penny held the door open while she settled herself in. 'All right?' she asked, gently closing the door.

'How's your mother, dear?' Mrs O'Brien asked when they were finally on the road.

'Oh, you know Marie,' Penny said. 'It'll take more than a spider to bring her down.'

'She's always been brave. Marie's the bravest person I know. I'll never forget her worried little face when we met her off the ship. All that way to the other side of the world, not knowing a soul.'

Yeah, yeah. Her mother was made of sterner stuff than she was; no question.

THIRTY

Love-longing

He took Janice out. He took Charlotte out. He fell into their beds as if falling into a dream, into sleep, into unconsciousness. He watched his body going through the motions; he watched himself put up a fight with Janice; a man of scruples, a man of principles and, besides, she wasn't his type. Her lips were wrong, too thin, too straight, her eyes too hard; he couldn't, after all, close his eyes and think of England. He remembered the crude adolescent jokes about putting a paper bag over their heads and going manfully on, but he found he could not go manfully on. 'I'm sorry,' he said. 'It's not you, it's really not you.' It was him.

He was surprised to learn that he was regarded as a mad rooter, a bit of a Jack the lad. Work colleagues thumped him on the back, joking about making hay while the sun shines. He wanted to say *do you have any idea what it's like? It's so tiring*, he wanted to say, *it's so relentless!* But he saw the envy in their eyes, the spill of something like wonder. It did not escape him, the paradox of men in possession of love, their eyes yearning, bewitched by the gleam, the dazzling light of unrequited desire. He was swimming in it, drowning in abundance.

She called him late one afternoon. He was on his way out to a work function, a drinks party for some mining company executives and the Department of Foreign Affairs and Trade, at which he was expected to sniff down work like a tracker dog. 'It's Anna,' she said, in her low, unmistakable voice.

They met for a late dinner at her hotel. It was one of those new hotels, dark, demurely lit, the decor deep reds and blacks, lots of red velvet like theatre curtains, embellished wallpapers, his idea of a bordello. She wanted to meet in her room; when she opened the door, she kissed him lightly on each cheek, French-style, and immediately returned to the window, where she stood silhouetted, a drink in her hand. Below, across, the city, the jewelled lights of office blocks and apartments. The adolescent reach of towers fighting to be the tallest, Meriton—skinny, elongated—the winner, the tallest child.

'It's like an Asian city,' she said. 'A smaller Hong Kong.'

'I suppose it is. It's hard to see the changes in the city you grew up in.'

'We used to come up to Noosa from Melbourne every Christmas. Oh, and once we came up in the September holidays to go to that world's fair thing.'

'Expo '88,' he said. 'The official marker of Brisbane's coming of age.'

She raised an eyebrow.

'It's how Queenslanders date the beginning of modern time, like BC and AD. Expo represents the dividing line between the old Brisbane, the old big-country-town Brisbane, and the new Brisbane, the sophisticated, cosmopolitan city you see before you.'

'How pleasant to have one big date instead of the press of a million little histories weighing you down,' she said. 'Sometimes in London I feel quite squashed by the past. All those people gone before. All those hopes, all those millions of souls hurrying home down the centuries.'

He looked out the window, at the bloom of light, at the radiance it suggested.

'Oh, I'm sorry, I haven't offered you a drink. I've opened a bottle from the minibar. Indulgent, I know.' She moved across and poured him a glass.

'Thanks,' he said, taking a quick fortifying sip. 'Brisbane's also home to millions of souls. Who knows how many Aborigines lived here before we arrived? It's just that they didn't have streets to hurry down.'

She smiled. 'I'm not all that interested in Aborigines.'

'That's not very PC of you.'

'I'm not very PC. I believe in men being gentlemen and women being ladies. I believe some cultures are superior to other cultures. I'm much more sympathetic to conservative Muslims than my father is. There's something deeply erotic about the idea of a woman being veiled to everyone in the world except her husband, don't you think?'

He looked at her, her excellent body transfigured by the light, her hair cascading.

They ate in the downstairs restaurant, ham from Spain that came from pigs fattened on walnuts; an excellent burgundy. She spoke in long, meandering paragraphs; her lips were red, swollen, and he watched them as she talked, trying to ascertain if she was a racist, a provocateur, if she was stupid. She had no process, no method, she was all over the place, a mind clearly untrained. It turned out that she had a soft spot for Muslims because she had for some years followed Sufism, a sort of branch of Islam.

'Charles led me to it,' she said. 'And now God has led Charles.' Her eyes filled with sudden tears. She sniffed. 'I'm sorry. I shouldn't drink.'

Jonathan leaned across the table, taking hold of one of her thin, beautiful hands.

'Oh, why are some people chosen to live this life of love-longing, Jonathan? Why did God pick Charles?'

He didn't know what she was talking about; he said nothing.

'I suppose some human beings are just branded by God, aren't they? They can belong to no other. No other relationship can fulfil them, no human lover can take hold of their heart like God can.'

Still, he said nothing. She was so beautiful. The light in her eyes was vivid, alive; the movement of her red lips, the planes of her face. Her voice was low, thrilling, rendering everything she said enthralling. She seemed to be talking crap, he knew that, some crap about God, but the way she spoke the words was so enticing, so dramatic, so dangerous and strange, he could not bear to stop listening.

'People like Charles can fall in love with a human partner, but something's always missing. However much the love of a human partner seems to offer, only one thing really matters: the heart's love affair with God.'

Her husband had left her for God? He thought that only happened in nineteenth-century novels or to fallen women in Ireland in the early twentieth century. Had Charles entered a Sufi monastery? Did Sufis even have monasteries? He was suddenly listening intently, pulling his eyes away from her swollen mouth.

She was tired, she was upset, she wanted to sleep. 'I'm sorry,' she said. 'Do you mind?'

Did he mind? Did he mind missing out on the fall into the abyss, that long plunge down? He was thankful to be held back from that smashed heart, from the train wreck that was love. Love was an enchantress, a siren singing him towards doom, a fatal cliff with nothing good at the end. He saw a picture of Anna's elderly, failing husband, inheritor of a castle or some such, some stately pile, silver-haired, frail, ill, called to God because human love was not going to save him, the love of a woman with swollen, inviting lips turned out to be no protection at all. She was alive, so animate, the first woman he had come across to have the spark of life, who seemed as fully human as Sarah; his imagination did not stretch to an elderly man choosing the love of God over her. The husband, Charles, was cutting her off, cutting off her son, giving everything he owned away: the grand house, his money, his goods and chattels. He said she could divorce him if she wished but England still had medieval divorce laws and what fault was she supposed to cite? Bad behaviour? Irreconcilable differences? Adultery? The other party was God. She could not believe it or accept it, so she bought a plane ticket with her credit card and flew all the way to the other side of the earth. She, who had loved Charles with all her heart, cast out onto the street—and by him, who had loved her, and so recently! Hadn't he loved her all the way through his skin, his flesh, down to his very bones? His skeleton was supposed to open its arms in welcome; he was supposed to keep the earth warm.

Jonathan, heading home to Southbank in the back of a taxi, thought the whole thing ridiculous; skeletons, renunciation, love beyond death—give me a break. How could ordinary, everyday love live up to its own publicity, to its own myth? He was sick of the unbreachable gap between idealised love and its puny reality. Yet he was moved, impossibly moved, by the mad human striving towards it, by the great stupid streak of hope, the vain, useless tilting. He thought: her husband is mad, and possibly she is mad too. A ghostly, silvery shiver ran over him.

THIRTY-ONE

Into her arms

There was a moment when Marie might have married again. Not in the first few years after Syd's death, which passed in a blur of grief, when all her grief joined up—her mother, her father, her brother, now Syd—when it took all her effort and will just to rise from the bed some days. She stopped sleeping then, her nights peopled by images of the dead, her mother's voice speaking to her as clearly as if she was in the room. *Who will save me from this misery? Why was I cursed with a daughter such as you?* Her father, weeping on the telephone from France, a telegram in his hand informing them of Eric's death. Eric's long-dead voice, alive again, the last story he ever told her going around and around in her head: German soldiers boarding his merchant ship at Marseille, impounding it and seizing everyone on board except—by some stroke of luck—him and Maxime Bodhaine, returning together to the ship with a freshly baked loaf of blackmarket bread. Plump, pretty Maxime, frightened, hopeless, and Eric, quick, out, away; Maxime never moving so fast in his life, both of them running down the docks and into the streets of the port, towards what looked like freedom and turned out to be one of the last unbombed ships crossing La Manche, sailing towards England, towards what they thought was safety but of course was not. No-one left! No miracle in the whole of her life except Syd, invincible, exempt from death, as if his leap from the bridge had turned him into another sort of being, one capable of transcending the banal laws of time and space. If Syd hadn't leaped she would never have been shocked out of whatever morose dream she was living in; they both agreed that his purpose on earth was to land, causing them to see the underpinnings of love and the way it held up existence. Not everyone needed to jump off a bridge to learn that, and not everyone needed to witness a man jumping off a bridge, but they did. It was their truth, the myth they lived by, and it brought them close, throughout the births of their daughters and the death of their son, throughout the years when he taught her the particulars of love, throughout the years when Marie inexplicably felt she might scream if she had to look again at Syd's smiling face. In the end, she knew she might scream but also that the face belonged to the only man on earth who jumped for her into the river of love.

The moment she might have married again came several years later, around the time Penny was attempting a new life in France. Possibly the two were connected; the idea of her daughter returning to that lost country, that place she could never think of without conflicting feelings of loss and shame. It was where her ghosts lived, her sorrows, her secrets; all the while Penny was preparing to leave she felt anxious, filled with a dread foreboding. Why couldn't the past stay in the past, instead of rising up and filling her blood like an infection? Why couldn't the dead stay dead?

She had many admirers. She was admired for her beauty, of course, but she was also admired for her wealth. After the worst of her mourning had passed—and grief never fades utterly but acts like a permanent deep bruise upon the heart, painful when memory presses—she looked around and got back to work. Her gloves were off, so to speak, and she set about learning everything she needed to know about running the business. Shop girls at McAlisters began to fear her arrival, her attention to detail unfortunately extending even to them. She became known in the buying departments of women's fashion, to the accounts department, to the men in the mailroom. She was a menace to everyone except Mr Stuart Middleton, the head buyer for ladies' fashion, who insisted Marie join him at special client lunches interstate at the Melbourne Club or in the dining room at Sydney's swanky Wentworth Hotel. At a function at the Greek consulate in Brisbane, he introduced her to the honorary Greek consul, a tall and handsome bachelor who had never married, who promptly asked later the same evening if she would grant him the privilege of taking her to dinner. She would.

The Greek consul was wealthy in his own right, from yet another family of Brisbane Greeks who owned properties, businesses and shops not only in Brisbane but throughout Queensland. Nicholas Anastas was impeccably dressed, with a cleft in his manly chin that gave his face authority. He was impeccably mannered, too, kissing her hand when he arrived by taxi to pick her up. He spoke excellent French.

She was flattered. She enjoyed being admired. She did not necessarily want to do anything with that admiration, or to have to act upon it; the admiration itself was its own reward. Nicholas was skilled at conversation, at drawing out enough information about her life to give them something to chew on. She liked having a handsome gentleman take her out to dinner; she was hardly old, only in her sixties, with many years ahead.

Nicholas never pressed her to go to bed with him. If she wondered why, she did not seek to address the question, feeling instead only relief that all that bothersome business was over. She had offered up her body once; she had learned everything she knew at the hands of her husband. She could not do it a second time.

He still lived at home with his mother, Demetria, high on a hill. Brisbane was full of hills, up and down like a drawing in a children's story, buses and cars and people puffing with effort, making their way up only to come careering down. After several months of lunches and dinners, opening nights and being his official partner at consular functions—the rich, handsome Greek and the rich, handsome Frenchwoman, sophisticated, apparently lucky, a formidable team—she at last received an invitation to meet his mother. She herself had not introduced her beau to her daughters. It was none of their business!

The mother was tall, like Nicholas, with an imperious manner, the daughter of a long line of aristocrats, a lost branch of Greece's deposed royals. Immediately Marie was on the back foot, as if the mother could see all her secrets. Everything vanished—her skill of entering rooms, of gathering herself up, of intimidating Australians. The mother spoke French, having been schooled at the Lycée Fénelon, one of the most exclusive girls' schools in Paris.

'What was your family name, dear?' she asked in French. 'Perhaps I know them?'

Marie blustered her way through, inventing, lying. Nicholas hovered, bringing Greek coffee in from a distant kitchen, bitter, thick upon her tongue when, in her nervousness, she mistakenly drank to the dregs.

'Maman,' Nicholas said, 'Marie's family business is McAlisters. You know, the department store.'

'Yes, I know it,' she said, making it clear from her disdainful expression she understood perfectly well that Marie came from shopkeepers, traders, men and women who worked for a living.

'Ask Caterina to bring in the sandwiches,' she said to her son. 'Don't get them yourself, Nicholas. She can refresh the coffee, too.'

When Nicholas asked Marie to marry him a few weeks later, she could not resist getting in a dig at Demetria. 'Did you get your mother's permission?'

He had the grace to look disconcerted. 'Of course not,' he said, though he had in fact been involved in several heated conversations with his mother about his romantic future.

'I'm afraid the answer is no,' she said. 'I'm fond of you, Nicholas, I really am. It's just that we are too old, too set in our ways. We each have our own lives to lead.'

'But our lives would be even better lived together!' he said, but she had already seen an almost imperceptible expression of relief on his face. It struck her that he was a man only interested in women he intuitively knew would reject him. She sensed that if she had said yes, he would have run screaming from the room. In understanding this, in knowing that there was only ever going to be one man in the world who would risk his life to win hers, she and Nicholas settled into sexless, harmonious companionship.

No more love! No more laying herself out, waiting only for the knife to the heart. If Marie experienced in life only one miracle, at least she had known one. She had seen a rare thing, a miraculous circle of love completed, Syd's first leap into life and into her arms and his last leap, landing in her arms. She closed the door on romantic love and turned instead towards the other kind of love, familial love, the love a mother has for her child, a love she had never known as a child herself but which as a mother was hers to claim. She knew it was magical thinking to believe she might wake to find disappeared Penny's dream of France, her daughter's quest for a French passport and answers to the questions she had begun to ask, her dive into the past, which had suddenly become troublingly inseparable from Penny's dive into the future.

THIRTY-TWO

Elsewhere

A French passport, a ticket to *elsewhere*, another realm of floating life, indistinctly sensed, dimly dreamed. Penny, at twenty-five, imagined an enormous shuttered window flung open to the air, the wash of sky. France was a soaring feeling in her chest, romantic undoubtedly—even preposterous—but that did not make the feeling any less enchanting. She saw red poppies, wet pavements in Paris, a girl, her, painting in a room. She loved best the paintings of the nineteenth century, Gwen John in particular, the human image painted over and over, a face, a mood, a fleeting human breath, breathed into blue air. She wanted to catch that breath, to live in it, her eyes looking out through the enormous shuttered window into everything possible, into every dancing second, every roaring moment. Oh, she wanted everything: to be the breath, and the girl painting the breath; she wanted nothing less than to join her exultant breath to all the other breaths of the world. She was mad to start, to get on with being twenty-five years old and full of breath, a girl with a passport to France.

She found out about Marie not through any effort of will, not because her mother suddenly underwent a change of character, becoming open-hearted and open-mouthed instead of closed, but because of bureaucracy. Penny learned the story of who her mother was because of the record systems humans live by, their wish to name themselves, to record the births of their children, their deaths, unexpected, expected, the ruins of their divorces. As if human life can be catalogued; as if the passage of a single life across time is anything other than a streak! A record of a birth, a marriage, a flimsy buttress against the monstrousness of infinity; a passport recording the movement of a man or a woman or a child through the borders of lands with mutable borders. *Pouf!* There goes Penny, clutching her Australian passport. But where's Marie's birth certificate, proof of her French birth, so that Penny might post it off to a nameless official and secure a French passport of her own? Where is Marie's missing life, recorded, written down?

Marie could not find her birth certificate. She acted strangely; nervy, unsettled. Possibly she was upset about Penny's departure, which she perhaps intuited as a bid for freedom. Marie had not been overseas herself since before Syd died, not since that last magical trip to Europe. Penny thought she might be concerned for her, remembering the strain of travel, the small, multiple exhaustions that come with being somewhere foreign that is not home. Penny asked about the missing birth certificate—again and again—but she could not ask Marie about her nervousness. She did not have the language, or rather they did not share a language of intimacy and disclosure. She sensed her mother's anxiety but she could not ask about its shape, much less investigate its origins.

The weeks were falling away, the days, the hours. 'What's the problem, Marie? You'll just have to apply for a new one if you've lost the original. I'll ring the embassy and get the forms.' Penny still didn't understand; not until right at the very end, only weeks before she was due to fly out. 'Look, I can't do it from France, Marie. It has to be done before I leave Australia. I'm running out of time!' Then, a new, unhoused Marie, a Marie Penny had never seen, helpless, exposed, an aged document in her hand, no words in her mouth. In her hand a torn birth certificate, written in browning ink, recording the city of her birth, Oujda, Protectorat de Maroc, in the year 1926:

Marie Azmiya Aréne

Pére: Hippolyte Santu Aréne
Occupation: Référence du fabricant
Âge: 29

Mére: Aicha (Emma) Aréne, neé Said ben Mohammed
Occupation: Tâches domestiques
Âge: 26

Marie wasn't even French! Or was she? She was something else, someone else entirely, and Penny's tongue was a stone in her mouth. Where should she begin? Where should she begin to seek the truth when her mother believed the truth was not good enough to be told?

'It's okay, Marie. It's okay,' she said, too embarrassed to look at her mother's stricken face, too mortified by her mother's mortification, her shame.

Penny went to the kitchen and made a pot of tea, her hands shaking, using the Royal Doulton teapot and the cups her mother always used, a wedding gift, still unbroken. She didn't know anything about Morocco, or why her mother would be ashamed of being born there. Did that make Marie an Arab? A Muslim? If her mother wanted to turn herself into someone else, if she could only live with part of herself annexed, who was Penny to object? Everyone made compromises, everyone lived with half-truths or old outgrown principles, some perishing set of beliefs that enabled them to get up in the morning. How many self-deceptions did Penny live with, how many evasions? She was in the middle of another unhappy love affair, with a man she knew was seeing other women, and yet she wilfully looked the other way. How much truth could anyone handle? Did Penny really want to know this man would never love her or that her ludicrous faith in art's healing properties would not necessarily lead to satisfaction; that she would never reach the life she intended?

When she went back into the lounge room with the tea tray, the faded document was gone. Penny poured the tea, her hands still trembling, her mind completely swept of anything to say. Back there, in the kitchen, only moments ago, she understood the situation perfectly and all the right words were ready in her head. Now, facing her mother, she was speechless.

'Mama never adjusted to Paris,' Marie said, her voice small. '*Jamais. Sa vie était finie.*' Her life was over.

Penny dared not speak.

'None of the other women would speak to her,' Marie said.

She wanted to ask which women but did not.

Marie took a sip of tea, a lone tear coursing down one cheek. 'She used to take us to Belleville. Eric. *Moi*. We weren't allowed to tell Papa. Her sister lived there.'

Still Penny did not speak, frightened that if she did, she would say the wrong thing and her mother would stop. It seemed that all her life she had been waiting for this moment.

She waited. She waited for her mother's confession, for Marie to unscroll her life, starting from the top, for the people and places and smells and colours and sounds to fall magnetically into place, like a beautiful equation solved or a perfect poem or painting. She waited for the inconsistency to be explained between our vision of life and the wanting, imperfect truth of living; she waited for her mother to tell her everything.

'Papa was from Ajaccio,' she said. 'Corsica has the clearest water I have ever seen.'

Penny waited. She took a sip of tea, which was already growing cold.

'I never learned to swim. Eric pushed me in. I nearly drowned.' She put down her cup, wiping her cheek.

'You have no idea what it was like,' she said. 'They never accepted us. Never.'

'Who never accepted you?'

'Where is my handbag? *Mon sac?* I need a handkerchief,' Marie said, looking helplessly around the room. Penny leaped from her chair and rushed into the kitchen, scooping up the handbag from a bench. By the time the bag was opened, the handkerchief procured, the cheek wiped, the moment for revelation had fallen away. Tears, leaking noses, the plainsong notes of everyday life rushed in to flood that soft discrepancy, that receding dream, that yearning gap that, wide awake, can never be filled.

THIRTY-THREE

Breastfeeding

Scarlett sat down the back of the bus, as if she were still at school. Hippolyte was on her knee and Ajax next to her; he wanted to sit near the window. 'Hold on, A,' she said, which was what she had begun to call her first son, because even a short name can be shorter. No-one ever called her anything but Scarlett.

Paul had the car and she had seen her mother driving off, fast, a while ago. Besides, she couldn't ask her mother to drive her into Tewantin. Her mother saw everything. Her mother was a bitch. She, Scarlett, was going to be a different sort of mother; she was never going to ask about homework and assignments and getting into university and doing something creative with your life. She and Paul were already thinking about Steiner schools or alternative education, or possibly no school at all. What was wrong with home schooling? What was wrong with taking off to see the world, two kids tied to your coat-tails, flying behind?

They would learn a lot more out of school than in it. She had heard that kids picked up fluency in another language in only a few months. Why, they could go anywhere!

And then she remembered her reason for sitting on the bus. She was still breastfeeding and no-one got pregnant while they were breastfeeding. She couldn't be pregnant. She would never fit into her wedding dress.

PART
V

THIRTY-FOUR

Home and away

Penny said she would be delighted to take Marie and Mrs O'Brien into Tewantin for lunch. 'But can you bear to go out again? You've only just arrived,' she said to Mrs O'Brien, who looked too defeated by the press of too many days to go anywhere. Penny knew there was a person in there somewhere, beyond the curved spine, the forest of bone and the sorry head, bowed as if in supplication, forced to look perpetually at the ground. She tried to picture herself trapped in an old person's body, and failed. She knew it was a privilege to grow old, she knew it was a dispensation from God, from fate, to be bent crooked and walking the earth, each working finger a mercy. Yet when she looked at her own hands, she saw hands grown dispossessed, ugly. She no longer liked looking in mirrors. She yearned to be like Mrs O'Brien: crooked as a storybook witch, oblivious to mirrors, catching trains, dispensing love.

The two old women settled into the car, Marie in the front (the better to tell Penny where to go and give her advice about road signs) and Mrs O'Brien in the back, her bent head nodding like one of those novelty dogs that used to adorn the back windows of cars. On the way out of town she saw Giselle again, darting through the bushes.

'You've gone the wrong way,' said Marie.

'No I haven't. I'm the one who lives here.'

'The other way is shorter.'

'Are you in a hurry?' Penny said, trying not to snap, mindful of the old woman sitting in the back.

'Oh, Marie's always in a hurry,' Mrs O'Brien said. 'She's been in a hurry ever since I met her. It's how she gets so much done. Look what she's achieved!'

'Hmm,' said Penny.

'She's driven, that's what she is. Driven.'

'Oh, don't speak such nonsense, Wendy,' Marie said. 'You always speak nonsense.'

'Marie! Don't be so rude!' said Penny. 'I'm sure she doesn't mean it, Mrs O'Brien.'

Mrs O'Brien laughed. 'Oh yes, she does. I don't mind.'

Penny glanced at her in the rear-vision mirror; Mrs O'Brien was smiling.

'Look out for that stop sign,' said Marie. 'And mind your own business, Penny. Don't speak of what you don't know.'

It was a gift, her mother's genius for alienating the very people she should have been drawing nearer. What was it about people that made them so stupid, including herself? What was it in them that made them smoke the cigarettes that might kill them, marry the wrong people, push away everyone they loved?

Marie suggested they go to the Royal Mail.

'But it's full of pokies,' said Penny.

'Knowing Marie's luck, she'll win,' said Mrs O'Brien admiringly.

The original wooden pub was built at the end of the nineteenth century, during the heyday of timber and gold, but the brick monster that replaced it after it burned down was a hideous mid-twentieth-century affair. It was peopled by the retired, by unemployed men who drank and smoked too much, by gamblers, fishermen and occasional holiday-makers.

'Look, there's a Thursday special,' said Marie as they drove by. 'Two for the price of one. Schnitzel with chips, sixteen ninety-five.'

Anyone would think her mother was an old-age pensioner, living from payment to payment. Penny gave up and turned the car into the hotel driveway.

'Three lemon, lime and bitters, please,' Penny said to the barman after ordering lunch. She could see them in the mirror; two old ladies, their walking sticks and frames resting by the wall, their heads close together.

Someone tapped her on the shoulder and she turned around. 'You can't get away that easily,' said Phil from the shop.

She laughed weakly.

'Having lunch?' he asked. 'I always come on a Thursday before I do the banking. Don't tell Sylv.' He winked.

The trouble with staying in one place, Penny knew, was that you couldn't hide. She couldn't pretend to be anyone else, someone better than she was. Living in a small community exposed you, made you vulnerable; she was Penny Collins, the mother of scandalous Scarlett, who used to be married to Pete, known as PP. She was the high school art teacher, too elitist to send her own daughter there. She had less room to manoeuvre than if she lived stranded within a foreign tongue in Paris or Rome; away, she might be anyone, but at home every gesture was recognisable, every signal familiar; at home she was doomed to be only herself.

'Did you hear young Jonathan has teamed up with Gordie's daughter?' Phil asked. 'She's down in Brisbane staying with him.'

Penny picked up the drinks. 'That was quick,' she said. She smiled and walked away.

'Careful,' said Marie as she approached, clutching the three glasses.

'I worked as a waitress for four years during art school,' she said. 'Never spilled a drop.' Just as she said this, she tripped on the carpet; only luck prevented her from dropping the lot. As it was, a fair bit spilled onto the table.

Mrs O'Brien laughed. 'Pride comes before a fall,' she said. Her mother said nothing, being engaged with flirting from afar with Phil. She was waving at him.

'Don't encourage him!' said Penny, hurriedly unwinding the paper serviettes from the knives and forks to mop up the spill. 'I don't want him crashing our lunch.' She was trying not to think of Jonathan and his easy grace, the way he boyishly ducked his head. Why was there always someone for a divorced man but rarely for a divorced woman?

By the time she refocused, Wendy O'Brien was halfway through a story; something about London, battered and smoggy in the fifties after the war, rationing, but *so* exciting, coming alive; her first day as a London schoolteacher, how petrified she was and how, before she knew it, she found herself telling the children a ridiculous story about getting her head stuck between the front steps.

She laughed. 'Now I couldn't get my head stuck if my life depended on it! I couldn't bend to do it!' she said, as if it were funny, as if it were not tragic how human life led in one inevitable direction. Penny looked away but her eyes were caught by her mother's face, and a small, unwilling smile on it that looked begrudged.

'It was most amusing,' said Marie. 'Most amusing.' Then she patted her hair, her eyes sweeping the room for admirers.

Like a coward hoping for safety in numbers, Penny brought up the difficult subject of where Marie was going to live. 'Are you still at Toowong, Mrs O'Brien?' she asked. 'I remember your beautiful garden.'

Mrs O'Brien's face broke open with pleasure. 'Oh, wasn't it glorious? I always wanted a white garden and Ken made my dream come true. Magnolias and white camellias and orange blossom and jasmine. It was heaven when everything was in bloom.'

'No-one needs a garden at our age, Wendy,' said Marie.

'I suppose not,' she replied. 'Ken couldn't tend it at the end. For a while Troy did it but he got too busy and we had to get a gardener. Can you imagine? It was dreadfully expensive.'

'Now she has no garden, which is better,' said Marie.

'Oh, I couldn't have no garden! I *do* have a garden, it's a communal garden, very pretty, and very well cared for.'

'Where's that?' asked Penny, moving closer.

'It's a lovely place out past Jindalee, in a suburb called Sinnamon Park. I'd never heard of it before. I wouldn't know half the new suburbs in Brisbane now.'

'Brisbane extends all the way down to the Gold Coast and nearly all the way up to the Sunshine Coast. It's like Las Vegas,' Marie said.

'What's it called, where you live?' said Penny.

'Sinnamon Village,' said Mrs O'Brien. 'It's run by the people from the Uniting Church. Before I moved in, Troy and Denise brought all my furniture and things so when I opened the door it was just like stepping into home! It was such a lovely surprise.'

Penny looked at her mother.

'But it is not home, is it?' Marie said. 'It is never home.'

'Oh, but it is! It felt like home straight away. You just haven't found the right place yet, Marie. Why don't you come and have a look at mine? I'm sure Penny wouldn't mind driving you over.'

Mrs O'Brien was a saint. 'No problem at all,' Penny said. 'Any time you want. I'm back at school next week so maybe we could go this week? Or next weekend?'

'No thank you,' Marie said. 'I am going to make instead a proposal to you.' She turned to look her daughter full in the face.

Penny felt a lurch, as if the floor beneath her feet had moved, as if she had known all along what her mother was going to say.

THIRTY-FIVE

Little lunch

Giselle had nothing for little lunch. She sat by herself, picking a juicy sore next to the mole on her leg. She looked for Dan but he was with a group of other boys and all the girls were playing a game together under a tree. In her lunchbox, which she had packed herself, was a sugar-free, gluten-free energy bar which she had taken from the cupboard, together with two stale rice crackers. She was saving these for big lunch. When she left the house to walk up the road to catch the school bus, her mother was still in bed. Giselle had seen a dead person and now she always checked in the mornings to see if her mother was dead. Her mother was not dead, but she was breathing strangely, loudly, croakily.

She wanted to ask Dan if he would go with her looking for magic cupboards around the school. Her teacher was reading them a story about a girl who entered another land through the back of a cupboard. She had already gone into all the cupboards at Jules's house but all of them had backs. All of them were ordinary places, for clothes, for shoes, old plastic bags, exercise equipment and suitcases. All of them ended.

THIRTY-SIX

Good news, bad news

Amanda said she would have the fish of the day. She looked too skinny; Jonathan could not remember young women ever being so thin. The accepted ideal shape for a woman was getting smaller and smaller; soon all young women would be expected to be the size of infants. Amanda's waist was ridiculously tiny; if he put his two hands around it his fingers might meet. She wasn't drinking.

'The Hunter Valley, please,' he said, ordering himself a glass of Shiraz to go with his lamb, even though it was lunchtime and a weekday.

'So. How are things, sweetheart? Work okay?' He realised Amanda never asked him anything about his life. She was still young enough to believe he was born when she was; for her, he had no real existence beyond her own.

'Work's fine. I've got a gig with an after-school program.'

'That's great news,' he said. He waited for her to elaborate, but she did not. He'd forgotten that conversation with his children was a question-and-answer routine.

'Seen Mum?'

'Yeah. When you and Mum are finally divorced, she and Cath will probably rush off and get married. Maybe they'll ask me to be bridesmaid,' she said.

Amanda was watching him, a sort of smirk on the face that was so like her mother's. He saw that she was asking for reassurance; through the smirk, the old fear, the desire for a mother and a father to be like the sun and the moon, irrevocable as the earth's turning.

'She won't get married again, sweetie. Not in a million years.'

Amanda looked relieved; she was a child, not yet willing to put on the harness of adulthood.

Sarah wouldn't get married again, would she? He recalled a dinner party, shortly before she left, with two gay architect friends, and an impassioned debate about the value of same-sex marriage. He recalled Sarah saying that marriage was essentially a patriarchal institution devised to protect the rights of men and why would any two women want to parody it, let alone two men? But Alex argued that was irrelevant; the critical point was human rights and gays should have the same rights as heterosexuals. If only Jonathan had listened harder; if only he had ears and eyes and a heart that would tell him everything, every secret sigh, every secret breath, every secret faltering step a person takes in moving away silently but surely from another.

•

Amanda was going to carve in ink upon her skin the name of her new boyfriend.

'I hope he's got a nice name,' said Jonathan. He was pretty certain the ink would last longer than the boyfriend.

'He's got a beautiful name. Raphael. That's partly why I'm getting it done. I've always loved that name. And now I've met the man to match it.'

He pictured her baby skin, unbreathed upon, her miniscule fingernails, the merest flakes, like slivers of shells. The tender envelope in which she came wrapped, still carrying some sacred scent, and now traced with needles, branded like a cow. He would never get it, the carving, the blood, the ink; once the province of hard men who went to sea, prisoners, low-lifes, and now the realm of privately educated, middle-class young women. She had a twenty-centimetre blue butterfly tattooed on her back and a ladder of tiny Chinese characters running up the nape of her neck.

When they had finished lunch he said goodbye, feeling vaguely unsettled. In his head Jonathan carried a cherished picture of family conversation, in which true words were said, their exact meaning conveyed. In this imaginary conversation there was perfect accord, perfect understanding. As he walked away from his daughter now he recognised there was not much difference between Amanda's yearning for parents as fixed as night and day and his own dream of a perfect conversation. He was beginning to think this conversation—indeed the cherished, idealised family to which the conversation belonged—did not exist.

•

Back at the office, Jerry knocked and stuck his head around the door. 'Do you want the good news or the bad news?' he asked.

Jonathan opened his palms; a gesture of helplessness.

'DERM are pretty keen on it going ahead. The DG's got a bee in his bonnet because the minister wants it. Good news is that they've got Buckley's. It's bullshit.'

'Excellent,' said Jonathan. 'I think.'

'The minister's a dill. He won't listen to advice from the department. Have you seen him? He's about two feet tall, totally up himself.'

Jonathan smiled. 'Sounds dangerous.'

'Mate, you know my theory about small men. Everything they do in life is compensation. Hitler? Five foot eight. Napoleon? Five eight. Stalin? Five eight. I rest my case. This bloke's about five foot nothing in his platform shoes. Lucky he's not in charge of an army.'

'Better not say that too loudly,' Jonathan said. 'I'm sure there's some anti-discrimination law you're breaking.'

'I'm an unreconstructed alpha male, mate. We're a dying species.'

It was true: for all his Labor left politics, Jerry did not get feminism, sexism or homosexuality. He equated Sarah's going off to bat for the other team with someone going insane. There was much in modern life which Jerry did not understand, much less approve. Jonathan feared for Jerry's daughters and sons, for all the tattoos to come, the wrong boyfriends, the wrong wives, for all the inevitable wrongness ahead.

•

The next day he called Anna and, just before lunch, they met and walked around the Gallery of Modern Art. It suited her, the elegant space, the blinding white, the amplified air. She wandered off and he watched her form, her grace, the effortless lines, tapered legs seamed to curved hips. They ate in the restaurant on the terrace; the air around them spicy, fragrant, perceptively changing from spring into the warm reach towards Queensland summer. Anna spoke in her winding, meandering paragraphs about Hartford House, where she had lived, with such tenderness.

'It was built by Latrobe, the architect who designed the White House. It's Palladian, in the spirit of Greek temples, which were never originally intended as human shelters, of course, but as houses for specific gods. Latrobe's god for Hartford was Apollo. His inspiration was the Temple of Apollo on Delos.'

He watched the movement of her mouth.

'Apollo's the god of hunting, you know, as well as the god of music and the arts. There's a beautiful plaque above the entrance to the library of him playing a pipe, wearing the skin of a wild beast he's just killed.'

He tried to picture her life of hunting and grand houses; a son with a French name at boarding school in the country. He took a sip of wine. 'You seem remarkably well informed.'

'It's only because I adore Hartford. I wanted to find out everything about it.'

'I thought those grand houses were all owned by the National Trust. Death duties and what have you,' he said.

She nodded. 'Most of them are. Various large chunks of the Hartford estate have been sold off over the years, but the family's managed to hang on to the house. Hartford's open to the public three times a year, too—to paying guests—and we always hold a village summer party.'

He saw her, dressed in white, walking on green lawns adorned with bright flowers. She was like someone from another century.

'The army requisitioned the house during the war. We had the library refurbished a few years ago—dry rot—and we found American cigarettes and army scarves under the floorboards. Once I found a Georgian doll in an attic room. Porcelain, beautifully preserved. It was like stumbling across a perceptible ghost.'

He could not say what compelled him towards her. She had no job, no visible means of support, and had apparently spent her adult life flitting from husband to husband. She lived in England, for God's sake.

'You remind me of Jean-Christophe,' she said. 'The same *tristesse*.'

He waited.

'Gaspard's father.'

'Is that good or bad?'

'Oh, definitely good. Jean-Christophe was the most sensual man I have ever met. Our carnal appetites were exquisitely matched. The trouble was every other woman also thought he was the most sensual man she had ever met. And he loved women.' She gave a hopeless sort of shrug.

Did she move her hand towards his, or was it the other way around? He looked down and their fingers were laced; he felt the warmth and softness of her skin, which lived in greenness, in mists, beyond the reach of the Queensland sun. 'We should make love,' she said. 'I'm tired of tears.'

THIRTY-SEVEN

Nowhere on earth

Penny had heard of grown women who lived in countries far from their mothers—economic migrants, say, or political or religious refugees. She had heard some mothers and daughters did not squabble over a daughter's life, as if over territorial rights, as if a daughter's life was a contested land. She knew mothers and daughters sometimes lived in the same country but in different cities, starting with her own sister. Her closest friend, Karen, the other art teacher at school, had an aged, widowed mother in a nursing home in Melbourne, two thousand kilometres away, whom she saw once or twice a year. Penny had long anguished conversations with Karen about mothers, but the anguish was all Penny's. Karen was pragmatic: 'My family lives here. My first commitment's to them. She knows that.' Did Karen's distant mother believe it? What sort of mother relinquished her own claim? Penny pictured Karen's faraway mother, selfless, speechless, like a bride of Christ in a silent, enclosed order of lonely old women, moving soundlessly down empty, echoing halls.

'We'll talk about it later,' Penny said.

'There is plenty of room—more than enough,' said Marie. 'I could have my own entrance. My own key. We do not need to build internal stairs.'

Internal stairs! Her mother winding up the stairs, into her life, penetrating even further into her existence. Marie's envelopment of Penny's life would be complete, her inhabitation absolute. She had recently read that an infant left in its mother's body traces of foetal cells, thereby ensuring their mutual DNA was forever intertwined. Whose body was it? Whose life? In biological terms her mother's body was a chimera, the house for every living thing it had created. Penny was still there, and Rosemary, and their dead brother, Eric, a tracery of souls. Was this why Scarlett leaped? Scarlett, effectively jumping from the window, making a dash for freedom, running off with Paul. Scarlett was possibly cannier than she was, following a blind, instinctive urge to save herself, leaping from the body of her mother's house, fast.

Mrs O'Brien was fine, thank you. She did not need anything for the journey; she did not need water.

'What is this foolish nonsense about carrying bottles of water?' asked Marie. 'As if everybody was about to march off into the desert.'

They were almost at the train station, with twenty minutes to spare. When they arrived at the empty car park, Penny wound down the windows; there was a cloying smell, like talcum powder. Perhaps it was 4711 Eau de Cologne? Yardley's Lavender? It was some scent from her childhood, from when she was standing at the same height as the dressing table, watching her mother dressing to go out. Her mother wore her hair in what she called a French roll, swept up in a glamorous twist; Penny watched as she manipulated the pins, clamping the ones she was about to use between her teeth. Her mother was a swirl of hair, perfume and mystery.

'Did you hear that old Peggy Burton died three times on the operating table?' Mrs O'Brien asked. 'You know—Peggy from across the road.'

Penny wondered how old 'old' was to an eighty-six-year-old, or whatever age Mrs O'Brien was.

'I cannot remember any Peggy Burton,' said Marie. 'Not even one who died three times on the operating table.'

'They gave her a pig's heart,' Mrs O'Brien said.

Penny laughed. 'Surely not. No-one's been given a pig's heart. Only bits of them—veins or valves or something—because a pig's heart is similar to a human heart.'

Marie, in the front seat, gave a derisive sniff. 'With many people it is hard to tell the difference.'

'You must remember Peggy, Marie!' said Mrs O'Brien. 'She had the most enormous bosoms. Ken used to say that one day poor Les Burton—he was only a little chap—would fall between them and never be found again.'

'I don't remember any enormous bosoms,' Marie said.

Penny rolled her eyes; she was still thinking about pigs' hearts. 'Didn't the hunter who was ordered by the wicked stepmother to bring back Snow White's heart give her a pig's heart as a substitute? Come on, ladies, we'd better get moving.'

She went around to the back seat door and helped Mrs O'Brien from the car. Marie insisted on getting out and the two old women embraced. As in a fairy tale, they said goodbye, their human hearts still beating in their old chests, their shared human moments gathering about them. They were witnesses to each other's vanished selves, each to the other representing a sum testament of lived experience. Was this the last time they would embrace, the last time they would speak of this and that, of pigs' hearts and forgotten women with enormous bosoms who died three times? Marie allowed herself to be embraced, and Wendy held her fast. To Penny's surprise Marie clasped Wendy hard, as if their shared past danced about their heads, hot nights in a wooden house on wooden posts, a set of matching luggage, two young women wearing gloves, a noisy schoolroom in Primrose Hill, two women of beating human hearts and numbered days.

On the way back to The Landing, Penny did not speak but kept her eyes on the road, on the twisting bitumen, all the while thinking about how she might extract herself or whether, after all, she should give in gracefully. What was she saving herself for? A man? God forbid—surely not Jonathan Lott? For her art? For some time now she had cherished an idea of turning the area beneath the house into a studio and now, since that terrible drunken night at Jonathan's, it was more than an idea, it was a sort of conviction. She had continued to paint—sporadically, unforgivingly, full of the usual doubts and failures—working in a makeshift space beneath the windows in Scarlett's old bedroom, but now she carried an impression, some faint image she wanted to realise, an idea which felt like a compulsion, the same charged, excited feeling she remembered from the years when she still believed in the possibility of making something good. Ever since that drunken revelation—her life laid bare, herself the architect of her own disappointment—her desire had hardened into commitment. A mother, or an artistic pledge? A beating human heart, or a pig's heart in a fairy tale? Who was she kidding? What were the chances of a middle-aged—no, older than middle-aged—of an *ageing*, older woman, rushing towards the future, bursting with excellence?

'I should like you to consider my proposal carefully, Penny,' said Marie.

Ah, yes, Penny remembered how preferable it was to talk in a car, sitting side by side, no eye contact. They could drive from one end of Australia to the other without once looking into each other's faces.

'I will consider it carefully,' she said.

'I will pay for the extension, naturally.'

'Naturally,' said Penny.

'Don't be smart, Penny.'

Penny sighed. 'Honestly, Marie, do you really think you and I could ever live together? You'd be telling me not to be smart every five minutes.'

'So?'

'So, it might not drive you mad but it would drive me nuts.'

Her mother gave a loud, theatrical sigh. '*Mon Dieu*. Where is this place where people do not drive each other nuts? It is nowhere on earth.'

They did not speak for the rest of the trip, not during the long curling drive down into the dark of overhanging trees, not through the flash of birds, swinging high overhead, not even when the clouds swirled, drifting towards dusk, blowing homewards.

THIRTY-EIGHT

This woman of many husbands

Who knows a body until it is unwrapped, the scars revealed, the mapped skin laid bare? Who knows a body's secrets even then? Certainly not the husband who lay for twenty-five years beside the wife, mixing their mutual breaths. Jonathan recalled the thin scar running along the length of Sarah's left wrist, from where she fell on a barbed-wire fence as a child. He knew her particular, personal scent, the smell under her arms; he knew the way their bodies fit together in a bed. She slept on the left, he on the right; every night she fell asleep, one arm slung over him, her face pressed into his back. After she went, he had to learn how to sleep all over again, how to lie alone in bed. For a while, he had to learn what it meant to be built of separate bone and blood, the awful responsibility of it. His sorrow was his, it was his decision whether to keep breathing or not, the stoicism he found somewhere deep in himself, a willingness to endure.

He had never asked her—and never would—if it was Cath who rose like the moon and him who sank. Perhaps it no longer mattered; perhaps it amounted to the same thing. If she didn't know who she was when she married him, then was it Cath who told her? Who was the Sarah of the many happy years of their marriage, when he could have sworn their bodies loved each other, worshipping pleasure's infinite dimensions? What happened to their sighs, their slippery joys, were they untrue, undone?

Nothing prepared him for the shock of another body, another mouth that was not Sarah's in particular. The first time he lay with someone who was not his wife it did not feel *personal*. It felt hallucinatory, weird, as if he had forgotten what his body was for, as if his body belonged to someone who was not him. He was returned to his forgotten fifteen-year-old self, to the oddness of the whole procedure, the importunate noses, the bra unfastenings, the mysterious panties. Her breath did not smell right; it was not Sarah's breath, and the wild thrashing of the act so exquisitely mirrored the wild, aching thrashing within his chest that he could not tell where the sighing and the flailing ended and began. He feared he was constitutionally, fatally, monogamous.

Anna's nipple in his mouth, the puckered pink scar in the valley of her body. 'A botched job,' she said. 'An emergency caesarean.' They talked the whole while, more or less, her dark, lovely voice, the cave of her mouth, his tongue inside. The act felt like an echo, too faint, a link in the chain of memories leading back to the ecstatic original.

Her head on his pillow, the streak of her plait, her eyes shining in the growing dark. 'I am made to be married,' she said.

'So am I.'

He kissed her again, this woman of many husbands, of meandering words. He knew there was a difference between someone who was made to be married *to the same person*, and someone who was wedded to the enchanting promise of marriage, to its beguiling idea. She might be made to be married to the ceremony of flowers and lace, possibly she was made to be married to it over and over.

All day at work, he thought of her. It was improbable, of course; she was a kind of mirage. She was not a proper grown-up person with a job and a line of steadiness behind her, a profession, a row of stable, civic years of staying in the same place, doing proper things. She had lived in Paris, New York, in a souk; she had married impecunious men, actors, unsteady types, men who did not even own a house. Owning property was surely one of the cornerstones of adult existence; he feared Anna naturally belonged to that rowdy crew who lived by their wits, surviving by the skin of their teeth, freelancers, contract workers, artistic sorts, men who inherited money rather than working for it. Her natural constituency was risk, that wide-open place of impulse, exhilaration and chance, of haring off down any new path that looked more interesting. How could an adult not have had a proper job, even a good-looking female adult? She was a throwback to women who were courtesans, kept women, to clever mistresses of eighteenth-century French courts. What would he do with her? How soon before she grew bored with him, tossing him aside for someone racier, more rackety?

When he came home he found Anna had been cooking, a Normandy bisque, heavy with cream, butter and Calvados, the prawn stock strained through a muslin-lined sieve; milk-fed veal, with tarragon. There was a pear *tarte tatin* cooling on a bench; the table was dressed, candles he did not know he owned in the centre, faltering in an unseen breeze. She kissed him, telling him about the particulars of the food, pouring him a glass of iced champagne. Where did she find a muslin-lined sieve?

'Am I supposed to be impressed?' he asked. 'Consider me impressed.'

'I had nothing else to do,' she said. 'And I love cooking.'

It turned out she was a magnificent cook, as if she had been spending her many marriages at cooking school. 'I helped out at a friend's restaurant for a couple of months once, in Soho. New York Soho, not London Soho. Everyone was a drunk or a heroin addict, just like in that book,' she said.

'I hope you didn't spit in anyone's dinner,' he said.

'Only in the dinners of people I didn't like. I wouldn't spit in your dinner,' she said, leaning over to kiss him. She tasted of cream.

He had a giddy, sprawling feeling in his chest, as if he were about to do something rash. He might fall in love; he might lay himself out, as if at a feast, forget his terrors about remaining loveless the rest of his days, his fears about tourists walking past his house at The Landing, the last place on earth where he felt inviolate, himself, free of his useless, leftover love for a woman who no longer loved him. It did not matter if the tourists came, if they trampled his soft lilies underfoot or peered into his windows. He could live with a new wife; washed awake, cleansed inside and out, himself turned transparent as a window. He felt alive with possibility, with crazed, unruly hope, even while he understood it to be madness. He wanted to be an idiot for once. He wanted to be rash, foolish, to really give them something to talk about, becoming the fifth husband of a woman blown in from God knew where, a woman with fine breasts and a plait down her back, which he would climb, as if scaling the soaring heights of heaven.

THIRTY-NINE

The blue egg

Giselle was beginning to understand stories. She was beginning to create links in the fabric of existence, to connect the material world with the world in her head and make meanings out of everything she witnessed. She was starting to see that this led to that, that a kiss might be evil or enchanted. If she closed her eyes tight, almost closing them, leaving a tiny strip open, she could see her trembling eyelashes and, beyond them, tiny dust motes or very, very small dots that joined up to make the colours of the world. There were millions and millions of dots joining up, millions and millions of people and stories, millions of moments that did not yet make sense.

She left fairy traps in the garden. Her fairy trap was a bower of leaves and frangipani flowers, a bouquet for them, scented botanicals so loved by fairies. She found a bright blue egg in the fairy trap, which she carried carefully inside and placed inside a plastic takeaway container, covering it with a cloud of cotton wool balls she found in a drawer in the bathroom. She let Dan hold the egg and she made him lie at eye level on the ground next to the fairy trap, dancing above him, casting a spell. Dan was an only child like her, with only a mother, no father, no brothers or sisters.

The blue egg floated in its spun cloud; the spell was cast.

Giselle was watching her blue egg when she saw the mother and the babies come home. Her mother was asleep again, on the couch in front of the TV, a half-drunk cup of coffee beside her on the floor and a pile of butts in an ashtray. Giselle's egg had a tracery of fine black lines running across the blue surface. Any moment she expected the egg to crack, revealing not a bird, but a fairy.

She lifted her eyes from the egg and saw the mother. Scooping up the container, careful not to shake it, she opened the front door and moved swiftly across the grass.

'Do you want to see my fairy egg?'

'Sorry, Giselle,' said the mother. 'Now's not a good time.'

One of the babies was crying. Giselle moved across to show him the egg and he stopped crying.

'He likes it,' she said.

The mother didn't answer; opening the door, she pushed the stroller inside.

'I have to get dinner now,' she said.

'I can help,' Giselle said.

And so she found herself inside. She liked being somewhere else, pretending to be a girl in a different life. Now, when the mother took the smallest baby from the stroller, she tenderly placed her fairy egg on the bench and lifted him up.

'Careful,' said the mother. 'He's heavy.' And he was, a giant head, as big as her own, rocking on a fat neck. His neck had rings of dirt around it. The baby smiled and pulled her hair. His breath smelled nice, of nothing, but also of something she could not quite name or remember.

She was still there when the father came home. The mother ran towards him and started to cry and no-one noticed Giselle. She watched closely: the crying mother, the crying baby, the father *sh-sh*ing and patting her on the back. She was used to crying, it was the background noise of her life. Tears burst from you, an internal font, perpetually full. Tears lived in your body, like blood, waiting to spill. The other baby started to cry; the mother, the two babies and Giselle, sitting there, half hidden under the bench, picking her scab.

She heard the word 'pregnant'. She listened to them talking, crying; she watched the father open a bottle of wine. She could see her blue fairy egg floating on the bench and she knew something exciting was happening. A fairy might appear, a blue fairy, matching the blue of the bluest sky, the blue eyes of the baby with the enormous head. She longed for it, for the fairy to appear, for the cupboard to open into a forest.

It was growing dark and Giselle hated the dark, the long, endless hours, the moving shadows, the scratching of trees like fingernails against the windows rattling in the wind. Every night distorted faces gathered around her bed; the breath of something foul upon her. She could not get up and run from her bedroom into her mother's room because there was something, or someone, beneath the bed and the minute she stood up, her feet would be sliced off at the ankles.

Every night she wanted her mother, every night she wanted to sleep with her mother, *please, Mum, I won't wake you up. I promise. Oh please, Mum, please*, and every night her mother said no. 'You're too old to sleep in my bed. You're a big girl.' But she wasn't, she was a girl shivering beneath blankets, her whole head covered, the tiniest hole for her nose. Even then, the finger coming towards the hole, the nail, the spike, the gleam of an eye. She was suffocating, boiling, imprisoned by her senses, her ears like a bat's, picking up sounds from the room, from the house, from the yard outside, from the road, the village, from space. She heard every sound in existence, every hideous yelp, every cry, every whimper, her nose inhaled every possible smell. Her burning eyes saw light through the hole, or rather not light but a lighter shade of dark, a paler shade of blackness. She tried not to look, she tried to close her alarmed eyes, but every time they sprang open, as if someone prodded her with a stick.

She was so tired, she was so scared, night after night after night. She hated night, the way everything fell in, collapsing, the everyday bright world of school and little lunch and big lunch and drawing with chalk, the way everything hidden awoke, coming alive. If she wasn't so frightened, she would leap out of bed, but she couldn't, she couldn't, she was condemned to lie there, suffocating, deafened by the roar, until she awoke and found darkness turned to light.

PART
VI

FORTY

Clouds uncovering the moon

'Tell me everything,' Anna said.

'Everything?'

'The story of your life,' she said.

They were entwined, back in The Landing for another weekend, seeing no-one, laced together over the balcony, looking down. In the darkness, the lake made a sound like children splashing in the bath. There was just enough moonlight to make out lilies dancing on the surface of the slapping water, the grasses and rushes waving in the wildness of the wind. The whole world was moving, rushing, splashing, passing. He felt poised on the brink of a decision, this way or that, he could not tell.

'I was born feet first,' he said.

She laughed. 'You know more about me than I know about you. Why don't we start with why you haven't got divorced yet?'

He instinctively drew back. 'Oh, it's a long story. Anyway, *you* can't talk. You're still married.' He poked her in the ribs playfully.

'Only in theory,' she said.

'Well, I'm only married in theory too. My wife's getting the divorce papers to me soon.'

'Your wife?' she asked. 'You still think of her as your wife?'

He didn't answer.

'She seems to have a lot of power over you, your wife,' she said.

He leaned over and kissed her.

It appeared he was now living with Anna. She was a sort of event, a phenomenon like weather, a stroke of fate that had happened to him. He did not consider himself a passive man, yet in this matter he appeared to be inert. One morning at breakfast in his flat at Southbank, he looked up, surprised to find her sitting at the other side of table.

They never discussed her moving in. She simply stayed, and he did not ask her to go. She drove his car back up to The Landing to pick up the rest of her things. Her wordly goods amounted to two suitcases, clothes, a framed photograph of her son, Gaspard—who looked uncannily like her—which she set up on a dressing table in the bedroom, and an old, dog-eared copy of a book of poems by Rumi, which she read aloud, lying on the bed, her head resting on his chest.

'*When someone quotes the old poetic image about clouds gradually uncovering the moon,*' she read in her low, lovely voice, '*slowly loosen knot by knot the strings of your robe. Like this.*'

She took his hand and placed it between her legs.

It was as if he had been hypnotised. She was the proffered apple, a sort of sorceress, a blessing or a curse he could not tell.

Jerry wanted to meet her; Will wanted to meet her; everyone wanted to meet her. His parents were dead so he was saved from that; his only sibling, Phillip, an unmarried doctor—whom their late mother always referred to as a 'playboy'—worked for Médicins Sans Frontière on a tuberculosis eradication program in Phnom Penh. Did Phillip even know Sarah had left him? His brother regarded Jonathan's life as insufferably bourgeois—the wife, the house in the suburbs, the children at private schools—and lived his own erotic and emotional life recklessly, taking up with young student doctors for several months or sometimes a year, or else sleeping with local women from whichever region he happened to be working in. He stayed with a woman for however long it took for the state of being lovestruck to fade, and only once stayed with someone for five long years, a coldly beautiful linguistics academic from Boston he met irregularly in hotel rooms all over the world. He was not made for intimacy.

Jonathan thought he might give a little dinner party; Will and his wife, Lucy, maybe Jerry and Eleni. His heart quailed at the thought of telling his daughters; they were not yet prepared to relinquish the dream of the family, as he was not yet prepared to relinquish their mother.

Anna insisted on doing all the cooking, so that he was relegated to being a sort of barman. She offered rillettes and small delicious bowls of bouillabaisse to begin, a perfectly judged, moist blanquette de veau, four cheeses, and for dessert a magnificent clafoutis, made with fresh plums.

'Where on earth did you get plums?' asked Lucy. 'I didn't even think they were in season.'

'I have my sources,' she said, smiling. 'But this is Queensland! It's summer all year! It's only spring and already it feels hotter than London in a heatwave.'

'Yes, well, that probably says more about the fickleness of London weather than Queensland spring,' said Will. 'We Queenslanders are proud of our winter cardigans.'

Did she fit in? Did he fit into her life, with its wild wanderings, its mysticism, its unloosed quality, fluid as water? How did you even begin to fit two adult lives together so that they happily resembled a whole? He tried to picture Anna's unknown son, far off on the other side of the earth, alone, in a room. What kind of mother was she? What kind of son was this half-French adolescent called Gaspar, in a room in England, his mother living with a man he did not know?

In the days following the dinner party, the report cards came back. A tick from Lucy: 'Luce reckons she's wonderful,' said Will. 'Good-looking, an accomplished cook—and bloody exotic.' And a sort of half-tick from Will himself: 'Yeah, she's all that, but what does she actually *do*? I mean, apart from cooking up a storm? What does she live on?' As for Jerry and Eleni, they loved her straight away because Anna cooked like a dream, because she folded eggs and flour and care into a pie, because love was just another food of the body, entering the mouth, the nose, the eyes and the heart.

He might have guessed word would spread, that Lucy would tell a friend about Jonathan's new live-in partner, that Jerry and Eleni—those gossipy Greeks!—could keep nothing to themselves. Jerry was already going around telling everyone about his almost certain victory over DERM and that small, ridiculous minister in his platform shoes; how he, Jerry, had discovered that the original boundary to Jonathan's property was now underwater. The lake was rising! Or perhaps the earth was slowly sinking, as all life must, all living things, all bodies, even bodies filled with pies and love. Climate change, was it? In one hundred years the water of the lake had fought its way to land, spilling onto the earth in a cunning creep of native rights. Was The Landing drowning? The earth itself? All those drowned children, buried in the graveyard, all that love, was everything destined for the flood?

FORTY-ONE

Peace and love

Penny was back to Tupperware containers of last night's leftovers for lunch, to girls wearing too much make-up being bitchy on Facebook to other girls wearing too much make-up. She knew this because Chiffany Taylor—possibly a mutilation of 'Tiffany' and possibly the worst name Penny had ever heard—came to her in tears after class, accusing Kaylene Knight of bullying her. Penny knew enough about Department of Education bullying protocols to know it was one for the headmaster, so she led a weeping Chiffany to his office.

Every night she came home to a casserole or a stew, something tasty Marie had prepared. She had to admit it was pleasant not having to cook, when her feet were tired, her voice exhausted from shouting—or from the effort of trying *not* to shout—worn out from looking into the vacant eyes of adolescents, which was like looking into the eyes of goats. Did any of them care about fashioning life into some semblance of order, of trying to shape whatever small gifts they had into something worthwhile? She could cry with frustration, or else fall too enthusiastically upon a student who showed the slightest promise or interest. There was one boy in his final year of school whom she secretly adored: Thomas Bellini, known as 'Merlin' for his fascination with the dark arts of the occult and for painting impenetrable, gloomy pictures of deceased maidens. He had talent, spark, and read everything she gave him; his hopes were pinned on getting into her old art college, which was now part of Griffith University. She wanted him to succeed where she had failed, while at the same time a begrudging part of her heart wanted it to be as impossible for him as it had been for her.

Penny and Marie had come no closer to resolving the question of where Marie would live permanently. The subject of the downstairs conversion into a granny flat swiftly became a no-go zone, since Penny made it clear whenever the subject was raised that she was deaf to it, at least for now. Might Penny have the upper hand at last? Might the power dynamic that had been the mainstay of Penny's life be changing? Perhaps—could it be?—Marie finally understood that she needed Penny more than Penny needed her? For Marie was all peace and love, getting stronger and stronger, her physical health improving by the day. Soon, the lump and the spider bite were forgotten and she discarded her walking frame altogether, taking long, refreshing walks around the lake. She was growing younger instead of older! She was like some weird species of super being, rising at dawn to eat fresh babies. Her mother was a freak, no doubt about it, but she was also a freak living in the spare bedroom of her house.

Gordie joined Marie on her walks around the lake, so Penny was spared that particular pleasure. Indeed, Gordie was such a regular visitor that he represented the first crack in the wall she had built around the idea of her mother living with her permanently; Gordie offered a reprieve. 'Is your mother home?' he asked, to which she started answering, 'Where else would she be?' Marie found Gordie charming, excellent company, and was reassured to know that he owned not only his own house at The Landing but two rental properties as well. With his financial stability assured, Marie could relax, knowing he was not after her money. What was money worth, anyway, at the end of life? They agreed they had done everything they wanted to do, seen everything they wanted to see.

'Although I wouldn't mind going back to Paris once more,' said Marie.

'Oh, Paris,' said Gordie. 'It's more like a mythical place than an actual place, don't you think?'

'*Bien sûr*,' said Marie.

Penny often came home from work to find them having a glass of pastis on the front veranda, conversing in French. Gordie's accent was execrable, worse than hers.

Meanwhile, Penny continued to work on her secret project in Scarlett's old bedroom. The light was good, as if it bounced shining all the way up from the lake, trembling and rippling. She was drawing Scarlett's babies, sketching them as they rolled on the grass, nipping each other like puppies, a tangle of limbs. Hippy's small white milk teeth were evenly placed in his head, and proving to be excellent new weapons. In the bright room she was making something of the drawings. She did not know what.

FORTY-TWO

Intimacy

Amanda rang him in a panic, having heard he was living with someone. 'Is it true, Dad? Is it true?'

He panicked too—he was unprepared—and rushed to gather his thoughts. 'Who told you?'

'Does it matter? Are you? Are you living with someone?'

'Well, yes,' he said. 'Sort of . . .'

She hung up. She hung up! His grown daughter acting like a child, as if he had done something wrong. He was practically divorced; it was her mother she should be hanging up on, her mother who had fled the scene, leaving a trail of unimaginable destruction. Divorce was not nothing! It was a wound, a hit to the core of not one life but two—more when there were children—an attack on one's very existence. Amanda was heartbroken, he was heartbroken; everybody's lives were capsized. He could not ring her back, not yet; first, he had to work out what he wanted to say. He truly did not know if he was living with Anna or if she was a sort of vacationing guest who would soon be on her way. And did he even want it to be permanent?

He knew he needed to talk to Anna. It was Friday, they were going up to The Landing again for the weekend; the days were growing wet, hot, the waters of the lake warming. He wanted to clear his head, to see Anna again in situ, as it were, with her father. He wanted to see how Marie was getting along, and Penny, those women of indomitable spirit, problematic, full of interest.

All the way up the highway, Anna kept a hand on Jonathan's leg. They had fallen into intimacy quickly, easily, possibly because both were so used to being part of a couple. It seemed to him that being part of a pair was the natural order of things and having a woman beside him felt right. He knew, of course, that he did not want just any passing woman.

'A penny for your thoughts,' she said, squeezing his thigh.

'Hmm?'

'What are you thinking?' she asked, in the manner of Sarah, in the manner of women down through the ages. 'What lies behind that lovely face?'

'Oh, nothing,' he said, in the manner of men. He could not get the right words out of his mouth. How could he possibly ask her—without sounding rude—how long she was staying, or what her intentions were?

'I got a letter from Gaspard's school today,' she said.

'Oh yes? What did it say? I hope he hasn't been expelled.' As soon as he said this, he realised he did not know the first thing about her son; he could be a drug-dealer for all he knew.

'No, no, he's a brilliant student, as well as being a very good boy. It's the fees. They haven't been paid.'

'His school fees?'

'They're ridiculous! His father refuses to pay them. He says I'm the one who should pay them because I'm the one who wants him to live in England, going to that stupid school. Jean-Christophe thinks Gaspard should be educated in Paris.'

He kept his eyes on the road. 'Who's been paying them then?'

'Charles. But now he's given all his money away they've fallen into arrears. What am I going to do?' She removed her hand from his leg; when he glanced across, her shoulders were shaking.

'Come on, darling,' he said, conscious that it was the first time he had called her 'darling'. 'We'll work something out. Can't Gordie stump up a few bob?'

She began to cry noisily now, sobbing. 'My son is in England, about to get chucked out of school, and I've got no money and nowhere to live!'

Should he pull over? They were in the middle of nowhere, cars zooming by at a hundred and ten kilometres an hour. He slowed, taking her wet hand in his. 'It's all right. You can stay with me for as long as you like.'

'As long as I like? That's not exactly a wholehearted invitation!'

What was he meant to say? Surely she did not expect him to rescue her by getting down on one knee to propose? He kept driving; he did not want to stop and get drowned in tears and obligations. Sarah never cried—not even at the end. He was unused to female hysteria, or possibly he had blocked out the sound of it. Amanda cried, the family drama queen, a heart-wrenching sound that pierced him to the heart.

'Oh, what a mess,' Anna said through her sobs. 'What am I doing? Why did I even come to Australia?'

He didn't respond.

After a while, her sobs grew quieter. 'I don't understand you,' she said.

'I don't understand myself.'

She laughed, possibly a little too forcefully. 'Oh, Jonathan,' she said. 'Why don't we ever ask ourselves the right questions?'

FORTY-THREE

Breath

Jonathan and Anna walked into Friday night at the Orpheus like a bridal couple entering their reception. Everyone looked up and if no-one clapped it was a miracle, or a mistake. They were shining, marked out by a good fortune which curled Sylv's lip. Phil saw it too, both of them hidden from the noisy throng, sitting under a dirty marquee pitched well away from the pub, with a sign reading *Quarantined! Beware, Smokers!* Rosanna saw it, and PP and Cheryl, who looked away. Even Giselle saw it, and rudely pointed them out to her drunk mother, who appeared to have also swallowed a few pills. Penny saw it, sitting at a table with Gordie and Marie, who were swapping pleasant reminiscences about Scotland. Penny had a tiger prawn in her mouth and slime all over her fingers.

'Sweetheart,' said Gordie, standing up.

'Hello, Pa,' she said, kissing him on each cheek.

They had a honeymoon glow, causing Penny to avert her eyes. 'Jonathan,' she said, as he leaned over to kiss her on the cheek, the same way he greeted her mother.

'Penny isn't it?' said Anna. 'I'm hopeless with names. Sorry.'

'Not that hopeless,' she said, smiling, lifting her cheek. 'Yes, it's Penny.' Anna was maybe ten years younger than she was—perhaps more—her skin not yet loose on her bones. Penny noted the graceful sway of her limbs, the twist of hair down her back, not yet grey, not yet telegraphing her exact position along the life span continuum of a perishable woman. Penny dyed her hair, though she could not have said why. She was filled with a prickly feeling, for Anna's ageless hair, for her loosened limbs, for her unconscious display of that happy unlocked feeling in the chest that followed sensual pleasure.

'Have you eaten?' asked Gordie, pouring them each a glass of wine from his bottle. 'The rump is excellent.'

Penny dangled her fingers in the finger bowl, then squeezed hard on a tiny useless scrap of floating lemon. 'I'm going to wash my hands,' she said. 'Only get the prawns if you're both having them. Prawn juice is not conducive to romance.' She intended this remark to sound amusing, but it came out sounding bitter. She hurried to the bathroom.

Two teenage boys came in, wearing head-to-toe black, walking far ahead of their parents, who did not have anything to do with them and their black uniqueness, nothing whatsoever. Scarlett knew what they were thinking, following them in, their woollen beanies pulled low over their foreheads, their legs trying to outwalk their parents and everything lifeless. She was being loved by her lover, Paul, who was pushing the double stroller into the Orpheus with one hand, the other slung around her pretty neck. The babies could sleep in their double stroller tonight, visitors at the feast, their place at the table assured. The new one in her belly, a sightless fish, might never see air. The babies already born could use their eyes to watch lovers dancing, or married couples fighting or else sitting silently together, nothing left to say. That would never be her and Paul! Scarlett saw her mother, her grandma, a whole pile of people, and grabbed Paul's hand, pulling him over. The whole cast, assembled!

The Orpheus was built of hoop pine and cedar, from the days when the forests were plentiful, when the lake knew its place and the waters of the earth were not yet in revolt. It had great verandas running around three sides, fixed with long wooden tables filled by the residents and visitors of The Landing, seeking relief from the rackety cover band playing inside the big central room that was once a concert hall, with its cedar windows and doors, its high, pressed-metal ceilings, the room where the dead once sat, alive, listening to passing sopranos. Now, there were no poems being recited but two electric guitars, lead and bass, and a passable rendition of The Pretenders' 'I'll Stand By You', the song that happened to be playing everywhere that first delirious year Penny was in love with Pete, the two of them dancing to Chrissie Hynde's tremulous vibrato in the first flat they ever lived in together, in Brisbane's Spring Hill. Look at Penny dancing now, skewered by memory, knowing Pete was somewhere in the room, listening too. The citizens of The Landing, gathered together, drunk to the music: the stoned hippies, the fitness freaks, the ramshackle young, dancing in the air spilling in through the open windows, alive to coming summer, which suddenly rushed in. There had to be dancing; there had to be limbs and hair flung about and a small feral child, Giselle, on the dance floor, spinning wildly.

At some point, Marie asked Gordie to walk her home. 'Your wish is my command,' he said, offering his arm. They walked slowly down the path—where was everyone? Dancing probably, only Anna and Jonathan left, canoodling down the end of the table. Out into the night they walked, the moon round and full, the sky swept of clouds, bright with stars. Wind frilled the air, picking up speed, beneath it the sound of throbbing music, voices and, as they drew further away, bats, possums squabbling in trees, far-off cars. Marie and Gordie, walking home, walking forward, amid the immensity of the world, its numberless blades of grass, its swirling air.

At some point, Paul started flirting with Anna. Scarlett could see it, the way he was smiling at Anna, in the exact same way he smiled at her! She was stupefied, filled with a cold, hard dread; if her eyes could not believe what she was seeing, her heart did, and it died in her chest. If she hadn't jumped up and fled, running down the road so that she and Paul—who ran after her—were not fighting under a streetlight far from the pub, it might never have happened.

At some point, Anna was left alone at the table. First Scarlett ran off, then Paul. And why was Jonathan taking so long? She went to look for him.

Jonathan saw that by some fateful bounce of a signal in space a text message from Sarah had been delivered to his mobile. Sarah! Her warm living fingers typing onto a phone screen—in Brisbane?—travelling up through the air, breaking the earth's atmosphere and ricocheting off into heaven, falling down upon him sitting at the Orpheus Hotel on a Friday night at The Landing. He was in the bathroom taking a leak when the text arrived; he rushed outside, not stopping to wash his hands. Would it still be there when he got outside? Or would it be swallowed by heaven or God or whatever swallowed such things, those virtual words, invisible, floating in space. He was rushing, half mad, trying to find somewhere quiet, in the light, so he could read it. He found himself in the pool room, noisy with the knock of cues hitting snooker balls; cheering. He stood leaning against a wall, holding the phone up close, squinting, blind with fear. *Please call, darling*, it read, *I need to talk to you urgently. Much love, S X*

Darling! Christ, he probably didn't have reception! Where were his car keys? Could he run back to the car and drive to wherever he had to drive to until his phone starting pinging with all those messages dropped from the sky? He rushed outside, still heading towards light bulbs, like a moth. Away from the veranda, just near the quarantined smokers, he saw that he had a couple of bars of reception on his phone. Was Sarah's message the one he had been waiting for? He dialled.

'Johnny?' she said.

And it all came out; how she had made the most appalling, grievous mistake; that she knew he would probably never forgive her, that he would probably never want to speak to her again. She loved him! She knew he was living with someone and when she heard, she knew without doubt that everything she had been feeling for months and months, the sadness that would not be loosed from her, the grief about everything she had left behind, everything she loved about Jonathan but had been too stupid to know, came flooding back. She loved him! Of course she knew it would be too much for him to take in right now, she knew that she had ruined his life and her own—to say nothing of the girls—but could he possibly, ever, ever forgive her? She did not love Cath; it had been a terrible failed experiment. She'd thought living with Cath would be different to living with a man—to living with *him*—that Cath would speak about her feelings, telegraph every mood, that they would live as if best friends, telepathically. It wasn't like that! Cath was jealous and controlling and she, Sarah, was miserable, miserable. Cath wasn't kind, like him; she wasn't sweet and full of tenderness like Jonathan, and Sarah knew she had made a mistake—she'd known for months—but she was too appalled, too proud, to admit how big a mistake it was until she heard about Jonathan and oh, God, what had she done? She was crying—Sarah, crying!—and then the phone went dead and he was crying too, which was how Penny found him, on her way to bum an illicit cigarette from the quarantined smokers.

'Jonathan!' she said, alarmed. She had not seen a man cry since Scarlett was a baby, rushed to hospital with a suspected fractured skull after falling off the change table under PP's watch. 'Are you all right?'

She had not noticed him holding his phone. 'Oh, sorry,' she said, turning to go. To her great surprise, he caught her by the wrist.

'It's okay, Penny,' he said. 'Please stay.'

He held her fast; with her free hand she patted him, awkwardly, in the same way she had patted a weeping Chiffany Taylor. How did you comfort a crying man?

'I need a cigarette,' he said.

'Hang on. I was just going to bum one.' She quickly moved off, exchanging two cigarettes for a dollar from two drunks. She handed one to Jonathan.

'When did you give up?' she asked.

'Twenty years ago,' he said. 'Sorry about this. I should man up.' He did not look embarrassed; he looked like a man in shock.

'Everything all right?'

'It's my wife. She wants to come back.'

'What?' She must have looked astonished.

He laughed, slightly hysterically. 'If it's a shock to you, you can imagine what it feels like to me.'

Penny took a deep drag, drawing poison into her lungs. 'I thought she'd decided she was gay?'

'It turns out she's not.' He was trembling; he had to sit down. His long legs folded beneath him on the grass.

Penny sat down too. 'Do you still love her?'

He shrugged. 'Of course. I'm a mug. But what difference does that make? Maybe that's the wrong question.'

'She loves you, doesn't she? That's all that matters. Take her back.'

He finished his cigarette. 'How? This has been terrible for me, terrible. From the moment she left I've been wretched. I've tried so hard to live without her.'

She turned her head up to the sky, implacable, fixed—for how long?—far from human stupidity. 'Oh, what a mess,' she said. She turned to look at Jonathan, a man full of love, and all of it Sarah's. Her heart felt strangely light, unburdened, as if it knew what it wanted. 'What are you going to do?'

He looked down at the grass, filled with suffering; everything within him had moved, altered; he no longer knew what to think or what to feel. How he had longed for her! How he had wished for such a moment! He loved Sarah—he still loved her and only her—but whether it was a compromised love he could not tell. Suddenly, he was conscious of everything: his legs beneath him, the dying cigarette in his hand, Sarah with her crooked mouth holding a phone somewhere in Brisbane. He looked up.

'What about you? What are you going to do?'

'About what?'

'I don't know. Love. Life.'

She smiled. 'You know, I don't think love's my problem. I thought it was love, but I'm beginning to see it's something else.'

'What else is there besides love?'

Now it was her turn to laugh. 'Aren't I supposed to say that? You're the man and I'm the woman, remember!'

He laughed too.

'Good. You're laughing,' Penny said.

'It's better than tossing myself into the lake,' he said. Did he feel a nudge of hope? Did he feel the beginnings of joy? He could not tell. Then he saw Anna, in the shadows, watching them, drawing conclusions. As soon as he saw her, he waved and stood up, but she was already rushing away.

At some point, Giselle noticed that the babies in their double stroller were unattended. Where was the mother? Why, she would wheel them all by herself triumphantly home! She would tuck them up in their beds, like a real mother, sing them off to sleep, show them the blue fairy egg nestled in her skirt pocket, wrapped in cotton wool. She had taken it out when she started dancing, placing it carefully on the chair, but it was back in her pocket now, keeping warm, safe.

Look at Giselle wheeling the double stroller down off the veranda, all by herself, her thin arms stuck straight out, her head down, nobody stopping her. She looked at the ground as she pushed, down the grass and out onto the road, pushing into the wind blowing down upon them, a giant's breath. The babies were so heavy! They were a weight, like great boulders, pushed over bitumen, over the crackle and rise of black bubbles in the uneven surface of the road. The wind was in her ears so she couldn't tell the difference between the cries of the babies and the cry of the wind.

Look at her, pushing the two babies, all by herself! If she looked down on herself from above—visionary, dangerous, headed for the lake—she might have seen a girl with a blue fairy egg in her pocket, dead flowers in her hair, a ring of browning frangipani flowers, a crown. A moment is all it takes to pass from this world to the next, for a blue egg to crack open to reveal a fairy. A whole life might turn on a misjudged moment, a jump from a bridge might go this way or that, a parachute falling to earth might land on the wrong side of the river in Pierrefitte-sur-Sauldre in the Loire, a pretty tributary of le Cher, a place for picnics, not dying.

When she rounded the corner, the wind changed direction; now it was behind her, pushing her on; now it was taking control of both her and the stroller, taking her elsewhere, the wind, like life itself, random, unguessed. She was almost at the lake, at the little landing by the side of the road, the waves dashing and leaping. She couldn't hold on! The thin bones that were her arms trying and failing, the wheels in the water before she could control it, into the soggy slime of the bottom of the lake, sinking. She was trying so hard; she couldn't push backwards, she couldn't push forward or straight, she couldn't see the babies' faces or hear their cries or hear anything except the wind pummelling her ears, her eyes, her face, pushing, pushing, and the stroller fell over, sideways, and the babies went in, into the waters of death. She did not see the mother running down the road, her whole life being decided by nothing more than chance, by nothing more than old busybody Sylv making a superhuman effort to raise her bulk from her chair to walk slowly through the pub to find Scarlett to tell her what she had seen, going as far as walking all the way down the road to the streetlight where Scarlett was standing beneath it, fighting with Paul; Sylv, obese, puffing, heroic. Scarlett, running faster than she had ever run in her life, her breath gone, reaching the waters just in time, wrenching the stroller upright, lifting her babies' mouths free of the flood, into the freeing gulp of pulsing, breathing life.

FORTY-FOUR

House of life

Jonathan did not yet trust himself enough, or Sarah, to make his way to a decision. Anna was gone, back to London, to mind the house of an old friend unexpectedly posted to Geneva for a year. Gordie paid one lot of school fees and Jonathan paid the next; an unknown young man called Gaspar was now the beneficiary of school fees paid by a man in Australia he would never meet. Anna was gone; a hardy sort of migratory bird, used to storms and hot deserts, and he felt sure she would find another spot to roost.

His daughters—both of them!—were badgering him to take Sarah back. How often does anyone get a second chance in life? It was their dream come true, it was his dream come true, a Hollywood ending. Yet, somehow, Jonathan was still wandering around the back lots, anguished, gathering his courage. He had been so hurt, so wounded, he did not know if he had it in him to forgive her. Did he want love's vastness back, with all its capacity for damage? One day he will decide, and his human moment—misjudged or correct—will join all the other moments in the fabric of existence, everything that did not happen, and everything that did. He will never know who Celia and Glen Quinn ran into at Lake Como, adding one more thing to the list of infinite things about the infinite world he will never understand, or know.

And Scarlett—no longer pregnant—will fit into her wedding dress when she marries Paul—with his fresh vasectomy scar—before flying off to Dubai, to travel in a four-wheel-drive convoy with her husband and their two babies into the desert, into the northern tip of the great continent of Africa, into the domesticated new world, where the names of shops on every high street of every first world city are interchangeable—Starbucks, Bang & Olufsen, Hermès. Homeless, at last!

And Giselle will grow up to finish high school, because of an exceptional teacher called Mr Leung, who noticed her. And she will eventually go on to become a schoolteacher herself, diverting the course of human lives as her own life had been caught, diverted.

And Penny will pick up her paintbrush in an ecstasy of release—painting the children who have vanished with their parents into the vastness of elsewhere. Here, with her mother in the next room—and possibly, just possibly—living in a new flat under the house, she will try to make whatever she is making, imperfectly and full of mistakes. She will take long-service leave; not certain what she is going to do with what remains of her life, but certain she is making something manifest, exploiting to the best of her abilities—or the worst!—her raw materials. She is herself, no-one finer. She might travel, or she might not; her project might come to something, or it might not, but, suddenly, she will be free of caring. She will see how far she can take a line for a walk.

But Penny will never be prepared for her mother and Gordie announcing one bright summer morning that they are getting married.

'Mum!' she will cry.

The light is fading, the waters rising, the scales waiting, mystically balanced between suffering and the radiance of love. For a dazzling instant, Marie and Gordie and Penny are alive in light's brightness. Ring the bells, raise the glass, for—right now—Marie is laughing, holding Gordie's hand, filled with nothing but the light of life and the astonishing words, *We're getting married. I'm afraid we're in love.*

Acknowledgements

Although a novel is written alone in a room, many unseen hands hold up a writer. For their warm-handed support I thank Emma Felton, Sandra Hogan, Barbara Johnson and, most especially, Jeff Humphreys, who not only offered practical and immediate support but also the most necessary kind of psychological support that allows a writer to keep going. It's been a joy getting to know Ross and Lyle Humphreys, both passionate, lifelong readers. My grateful appreciation to all those whose own work allowed me to construct a work of fiction accurate in its details—or at least as true as I could make it—especially Bede King of Tobin King Lateef, for his excellent legal advice on land fronting water; photographer Trevor Newman and his wonderful site about historical Brisbane (www.yourbrisbanepastandpresent.com) and for his childhood memories of Brisbane, and Dr Douglas Wilkie from the University of Melbourne, for his research into the French in Australia. I am very grateful to my employers at the *Courier-Mail* for allowing me the time off, especially Chris Dore, Peter Gleeson and Kylie Lang. I am lucky to have two fine fiction writers at *Qweekend* magazine as colleagues: Matthew Condon and Frances Whiting, and to Matt in particular I owe a great deal—I wouldn't have a job in journalism without him. As ever, my publishers—one of the last independent publishers in Australia and one of the finest—have been stalwarts, in particular Annette Barlow. Editor Ali Lavau's suggestions were exceptionally fine, as were Christa Munns'. My new agents Benython Oldfield and Sharon Gallant of Zeitgeist Media are wonders (as agents as well as readers). My most heartfelt thanks to the Australia Council for giving me the great gift of time.